P9-CSC-937

THE Angel of Forest Hill

Books by Cindy Woodsmall

Fiction

Amish Christmas at North Star

Christmas in Apple Ridge

The Sound of Sleigh Bells

The Christmas Singing

The Dawn of Christmas

THE Angel of Forest Hill

CINDY
WOODSMALL

WATERBROOK

THE ANGEL OF FOREST HILL

All Scripture quotations are taken from the King James Version.

The characters and events in this book are fictional, and any resemblance to actual persons or events is coincidental.

Hardcover ISBN 978-1-60142-705-2
eBook ISBN 978-1-60142-706-9

Cover design by Mark D. Ford; photography by Sandra Cunningham | Trevillion Images

Published in the United States by WaterBrook, an imprint of the Crown Publishing Group, a division of Penguin Random House LLC, New York.

WATERBROOK® and its deer colophon are registered trademarks of Penguin Random House LLC.

Library of Congress Cataloging-in-Publication Data
Names: Woodsmall, Cindy, author.
Title: The angel of Forest Hill : an Amish Christmas romance / Cindy Woodsmall.
Description: First edition. | Colorado Springs, Colorado : WaterBrook, 2016.
Identifiers: LCCN 2016026788 (print) | LCCN 2016033154 (ebook) | ISBN 9781601427052 (hardcover) | ISBN 9781601427069 (ebook) | ISBN 9781601427069 (electronic)
Subjects: LCSH: Amish—Fiction. | Christmas stories. | BISAC: FICTION / Romance / Contemporary. | FICTION / Christian / Romance. | GSAFD: Christian fiction. | Love stories.
Classification: LCC PS3623.O678 A85 2016 (print) | LCC PS3623.O678 (ebook) | DDC 813/.6—dc23
LC record available at https://lccn.loc.gov/2016026788

Printed in the United States of America
2016—First Edition

10 9 8 7 6 5 4 3 2 1

To Shannon Marchese, my remarkable editor,
happy ten-year anniversary!
For a decade you've drawn out the very best from my meager talent.
You've been patient and steadfast in ways readers couldn't imagine.
You've helped me navigate much more than story lines and deadlines—
from joyous life events to grievous ones.
Time and again you've blessed me with my favorite part—
long, thought-provoking conversations about each story line,
where you share insights and parts of your heart
so I can better understand life and love and loss,
all in hopes of giving readers
the very best we have to offer with each story.
Thank you.

Rose clutched the wooden handles of her embroidered traveling bag, tightening her grip to stop her fingers from trembling. Why had she agreed to do this? She glanced at the hired driver before returning her attention to the view through the car window. Since getting in this car almost five hours ago, she'd watched as the familiar rolling farmlands of Pennsylvania had given way to the mountains of West Virginia. The tree-covered mountainsides were majestic, with every shade of gold and red foliage, but as night overtook the golden wash of the fall day, the beauty was silhouetted by the darkness.

The driver, a woman who looked to be the same age as Rose's *Mamm,* lowered the volume of the radio. "There's a restaurant ahead of us. We can stop if you need to."

"I'm fine now. Thank you." That wasn't true, but Rose would fight her nausea rather than give in to it again. Since leaving her house, they had already stopped at three places to give Rose a chance to get out, gulp in crisp air, and press a damp cloth to her lips.

The driver nodded and turned the radio up, continuing to listen as men discussed how to fix the country.

It seemed odd that there was no one around to criticize Rose for letting time melt away as she just sat here, thinking. She let her thoughts trail back to earlier in the day, when her life was a steady routine of hard work and familiar safety.

She and her Mamm had been getting breakfast on the table—a vat of steamy, brown-sugar oatmeal and panfuls of oven-toasted bread—when Nat Eash knocked on the back door. Her *Daed* welcomed him and invited him to join them at the table.

Rose grabbed a mug and poured coffee for him and then returned to ladling oatmeal into bowls for her eleven brothers. Her parents were dairy farmers, and she was the lone daughter of the twelve children. Work never stopped, not even when it was Christmas Day or when she was recovering from the flu that had landed her Mamm in the hospital.

The bishop studied her as he sipped his coffee. Finally he

cleared his throat. "Hard times come to all of us, and we must help carry one another's burdens. The Forest Hill community is a small Amish district—only eight families—and they need our help."

Had she ever heard of that community before? She tried to recall as she filled a bowl with oatmeal and held it out to her youngest brother.

"Do you know where Forest Hill is, Rose?" Nat asked.

The bishop's direct question to her caught her off guard, and she dropped the oatmeal. Her Mamm and brothers yelling at her unnerved her even more, and her face afire, she was unable to find her voice.

Nat winced. "It's my fault. Not hers."

The complaining immediately ceased, and the bishop continued talking about the Forest Hill community and the needs of the strangers who lived there. A young woman had given birth but wasn't doing well, and she had two other small children. Like many in rural Appalachia, the families in the district were facing hardships, and none of them could move in and help take care of three little ones.

While Rose served her brother a fresh bowl of oatmeal and cleaned up the spill, Nat described the strangers' needs. But with her rattled nerves and her ongoing prayers, she barely heard him. *Dear God, if it's not a bother, show me what to do, and let Your truth set me free.*

"So"—the bishop stood, head angled—"would you be willing to do this?"

She looked to her Daed for some clue as to what the man wanted and what answer she should give.

Her Daed nodded. "She will."

Nat's smile hinted of gratefulness, but he also seemed a bit reluctant. Had he hoped she would be allowed to make her own decision? "I'll have a driver pick you up as soon as possible." He placed his fingers on the table as if steadying himself. "When the call for help went out to all the districts, I immediately thought of you, Rose, knowing the family couldn't find anyone better suited."

Confusion pummeled her. Had she nodded in agreement? She couldn't remember, but the next thing she knew, she was in her bedroom, and her Mamm was packing the traveling bag. "You listen to me, Rose Kurtz." Mamm jerked clothes off the hangers and shoved them into the bag. "You mind your tongue and do as you're told. I won't have you being an embarrassment. They have no idea how absent minded you are. Do you understand me?"

"Where am I going, Mamm?" Rose sounded more like a child than a twenty-one-year-old woman. Truth be told, she usually felt like a child—unsure of herself, clueless, and with little say about her life.

Her Mamm pursed her lips, looking torn between anger

and sadness. "West Virginia, where, I guess, you'll spend a month helping to look after this family's two toddlers and newborn." Her Mamm grabbed underwear from the drawer and thrust it on top of the clothes. "The bishop didn't need to talk about how suited you are for this. That's nonsense. There simply isn't anyone else. Most girls old enough to leave home and do this are married or have someone they're unwilling to part from for a month." She put her hands on her hips and sighed. "I have no idea what I'm supposed to do with eleven sons to feed and no help. I guess that doesn't matter to anyone."

Did her Mamm consider how unnerving it was for Rose? She'd hardly been outside of Perry County, let alone out of state.

"Rose," Daed called, "the driver is here."

Mamm shut the traveling bag and held it out. "Go, and remember what I said."

Without so much as a hug or an "I'll miss you" from anyone, Rose got into the vehicle.

A car horn startled her. Rose opened her eyes and sat upright.

"Sorry. Didn't mean to hit the horn, but we're here." She turned onto a driveway.

Even through the darkness of a fall evening, she could tell

that the two-story home was fairly new. It seemed contemporary and custom-built and surprisingly stately for an Amish home. The familiar golden light of candles and lanterns poured through every window, and a dozen buggies were parked in the yard.

Nat had said the community was quite small—only eight families. If that was true, every one of them had to be here. If the woman of the house was incapacitated after giving birth during the wee hours of the morning, why had all these people come to her house? It didn't seem normal.

The driver turned off the car, staring at the house too. "This is it."

Rose craned her neck, looking at the second story of the house and wishing she didn't feel so uncomfortable and unsure of herself.

The driver unlocked the doors to the vehicle. "When your bishop called, requesting that I drive you here, I asked about the situation. Let me say that what you're doing—walking into a stranger's home and offering to help—is admirable. It's a tough situation. Young children will want only their mama. But I'm sure it'll be fine. You seem like a hardworking young lady."

Why was the driver, who'd said fewer than ten sentences in the last six hours, telling her how hard the next month would be? Rose was Amish, and the Amish knew how to buck up and get things done. Always. What difference did it make how difficult the time would be? Or did this woman know something Rose didn't?

Rose opened the car door, thanked the driver, and then held on tightly to her traveling bag as she walked up the porch stairs. A baby was wailing, the most pitiful cry Rose had ever heard.

As she lifted her hand to knock, an unfamiliar darkness settled over her, like a mist shrouding her, and the hair on the back of her neck stood on end. She drew a deep breath and knocked. The door opened, and a gray-haired woman carrying a lit candle in a metal candleholder stared back at Rose. The candle fluttered and threatened to go out. The woman seemed mute, and tears ran down her face as the candleholder shook.

The home seemed to rumble with hoarse voices and muted sobs. Rose didn't want to be here. She turned and looked behind her, hoping the driver was coming in too. Instead she saw bright brake lights as the car pulled out of the driveway.

Rose drew a deep breath, hoping to respond the way a mature young woman should. "I'm Rose." She held up her traveling bag. "My bishop asked me to help look after the children."

"*Ach, ya,* of course that's who you are." The woman backed away. "I'm sorry. We . . . we aren't functioning well right now."

"I understand." Rose entered the home and closed the door. Despite the lit lanterns and candles, dimness filled the empty spaces in the large kitchen, living room, and dining area. Adults milled about. A few younger people were huddled on couches in the living room. Somewhere in the house an infant wailed.

A man sat in a chair with two crying children clinging to him. *"Ich will mei Mamm!"* The older boy, maybe three, cried over and over that he wanted his Mamm. The younger child, who was maybe two, cried loudly, as did the infant Rose had yet to spot.

Rose's heart sank. Had the young Mamm died? Or maybe she'd had a home birth and was now in the hospital. But wouldn't the baby be with her?

The man held the boys tight. *"Es iss allrecht. Es iss. Ich promise."* As he kissed their heads and promised that everything would be all right, he noticed her for the first time. When their eyes connected, she knew without any doubt . . . His wife was dead, and he was shattered. She doubted he would remember this night or any other for a very, very long time. Grief had a way of enveloping a person's mind and memory like a thick fog, and most of what happened while a person was inside that fog would be lost in the mist. Or at least that's what her grandmother had told her.

An older woman entered the room, bouncing the screaming infant. Rose didn't know a lot about many things, but that was the cry of a very hungry infant. She turned to the woman who'd opened the door. "How long ago did the Mamm pass?"

"She left here in an ambulance at noon and died within the

hour. I don't understand it. She was fine for a while after the baby arrived. As soon as she showed the first sign of hemorrhaging, Joel called an ambulance. They rushed her to surgery, and we were sure they'd save her, but . . ."

"I'm sorry." Rose wished there were better words at times like this, ones that could bring real comfort.

"Denki." The woman gestured toward the baby. "We've tried to feed her, using every kind of man-made nipple and formula, but she's refused all of it."

Dear God, if it's not a bother, show me what to do, and let Your truth set me free.

Possible solutions poured into Rose's brain, and she knew what needed to be tried next. "Is there a phone nearby?"

The woman nodded toward the front door. "There's a rotary phone in Joel's workshop." She took a shaky breath. "I'm Sarah Dienner, Joel's Mamm. What did you say your name was?"

"Rose. Rose Kurtz from Perry County, Pennsylvania." Rose set her bag on the floor in an out-of-the-way nook. An *Englisch* neighbor that Rose occasionally helped with laundry was involved with the La Leche League. If anyone could put Rose in contact with someone near here who could provide clean breast milk, that woman could. "If I could get breast milk and a special kind of bottle, would there be any objection?"

Sarah drew a ragged breath. "You do what you need to, and

I'll see to it that everyone backs you." She broke into sobs. "Grace's needs must be cared for. I . . . I'm not sure any of us, Joel most of all, can survive another loss."

Rose's moment of confidence disappeared as quickly as it had come. She could mess up pouring milk on cereal. What did she know about newborns, especially one without a Mamm? Rose could picture her own mother wagging a finger in Rose's face and telling her how miserably she had failed. But this loss would have much greater consequences than just another blow to her self-esteem.

With a pivot tool in hand, Joel stood at the bench in his workshop. The brass inner workings of a mantel clock stared back at him. It had belonged to Florence's great-great-great-grandmother, and his wife had cherished it. A few hours ago he'd noticed it had stopped working, and he immediately brought it out here. But he couldn't fix it. His eyes burned from trying to focus on the small cogwheels and to line them up as needed.

Night had fallen, and two lanterns flickered near him, giving decent light to work by. The cogwheels were stacked close to one another, and it took a lot of gears to make the clock tick. If one wheel didn't connect just right with another, the clock couldn't run. He set the tool aside and looked out the window, seeing pitch black. What day was it? How long had it been since they'd buried Florence? Thoughts of her being in the ground were driving him crazy. She should be in their home, the one they'd begun building their second year of marriage, and she should be sitting in their bed, glowing from the birth of their newborn daughter and hugging on their sons.

Light from a lantern moved across the lawn and floated toward the workshop.

"Joel?" Daed called.

Joel opened the door.

"Here." Daed held out a canvas bag. "We need to talk."

Joel took the bag and put it on the workbench.

Daed set the lantern next to it. "This seemed like the best place to say what needs to be said."

Guilt overrode Joel's grief for a moment. What was he doing out in his shop, tinkering with a broken wedding gift, while others were caring for his children? He had been helpful most of the day, hadn't he? Remembering anything seemed impossible. Were his children okay? Could he even help? "I should be in the house, helping. Sorry, Daed."

"It's okay. All of us understand. This has been a shock to the whole community, and we're not strangers to difficult times." Daed pulled a thermos, two mugs, and a few packets of sugar out of the canvas bag. "But here's the situation. It's been a week since Florence passed, and we have to return to tending our own homes and families. Your Mamm and Florence's Mamm want to be with the children and be of service, but they can't continue staying here like this. The girl's here helping, but decisions have to be made, Son."

For days Joel had felt as if he were flattened and spinning through endless dark space, but his Daed wanted him to make decisions? What girl? "I can't. Not now."

"I'm sorry, Son." Daed poured coffee from the thermos into one mug. "Things have changed, and we have to come up with a plan now."

"How? My ability to reason, to think, is gone."

"If Florence ever needed anything from you, this is it. Since she's not here to say so, I am."

Joel closed his eyes, seeing Florence standing before him, asking—maybe begging—him to pull it together enough to do whatever Daed needed. "Okay." He drew a deep breath, willing himself to do anything she would want done. "So what's going on?"

"Erma's rheumatism has flared up worse than ever, maybe from the grief of losing her daughter. But whatever the cause, she can't even get out of bed right now, let alone tend to your little ones."

Erma hadn't come to the house in several days, but he'd thought she needed time alone, like he did.

Daed started to pour coffee into the empty mug.

Joel put his hand over the cup and shook his head. "I . . .

I'm sorry. I didn't realize . . ." It would break Florence's heart to know her Mamm was suffering so.

Daed cupped his large, callused hands around the hot mug. "Your Mamm wants to be here for you. She does, but she can't leave your uncle Wayne at home alone for so much of the day. Johnny Yoder came to the house and sat with him this last week, but he can't continue to do that. I think the most she'll be able to come is a couple of hours a day."

"Only a couple of hours?" Joel sat on a stain-spattered barstool. How was he supposed to care for a newborn if his Mamm couldn't come for more than two hours a day? At the same time he knew she couldn't leave her brother Wayne, who at fifty-four had begun suffering from early dementia and had been living with Joel's parents ever since.

Daed grabbed a stool from a corner of the wood shop and set it next to Joel's.

"Your Mamm and Erma can't continue to help like we talked about when Florence passed. We have the girl from Pennsylvania for a couple more weeks, but I haven't found any woman in the Amish community who can leave her family regularly to help."

If Mamm and Erma weren't up to the round-the-clock task of caring for a newborn, a toddler, and a preschooler, who was?

"The girl from Perry County . . ." Joel stammered, trying to recall her name. It was ridiculous that he struggled to remember it. He'd spoken to her a couple of times, thanking her for helping. He'd seen her dozens of times a day as she tended to Grace and helped with the boys. He and the girl had kept a midnight vigil a couple of times—her rocking Grace while he held his boys so they could sleep. "Rose." So what was her last name? "She's good with them, isn't she?"

It seemed to Joel that she was, but maybe he was seeing what he needed to. Truth be told, even when he was in the same room as Rose, he was aware of very little except his motherless children and the ripping pain of grief inside him.

"Ya, she is," Daed said, "but she can't stay here."

Joel longed for the warmth and love that used to define his home, his life. He missed Florence so much it was as if someone were constantly cutting out his heart with no anesthesia. He pressed the palms of his hands against his eyes, trying to keep the tears at bay. "If . . . if we talked to Rose's bishop and her Daed, maybe they would understand."

"They aren't going to let her stay in your home *with you,* especially not at night. But you do need help. Your newborn and the boys wake and need some sort of tending every few hours. Imagine working a day after that."

He nodded. His two-year-old, Levi, had never slept through the night. Often he was up as much as he was down. Mose, his three-year-old, had slept decently enough before last week. Now he woke frequently, searching for his Mamm.

Daed sipped his coffee as if they were having one of their typical conversations about business and work load. "You need help for the next three to four years at least. Then some of the teen girls will be old enough to work for you during the day. Six years would be best. All three will be in school then."

Joel couldn't imagine enduring the next month, let alone years. He was twenty-nine years old, and instead of thriving, everything ahead would be a matter of survival. "Beth invited us to move in with her. Maybe that's the best option."

Daed's brows furrowed. "Your sister lives four hundred miles away and has a huge family of her own. God made you the linchpin for this community, Joel. Your business employs more than half the men here, and the elders have poured twenty years of hard work into establishing Forest Hill as a viable Amish community. What happens if you leave?"

Joel knew his value to the Amish of Forest Hill. Shortly after he and Florence were married, he connected with an *Englischer* in Hinton who taught Joel how to use his woodworking abilities to craft custom wooden canoes. With the increased tourism in their county and his Englisch buddy's help in setting up an online business, Joel's canoes were quickly in demand. It was a high-end product, and he added staff from the community to meet the needs. He hadn't considered what would happen if he left. The elders, including Joel's Daed, had moved here when Joel was nine because there was little affordable land in the Amish communities in the East. The men had been farmers, and they had thought they could farm here too, but the terrain was too different from Pennsylvania, and they had been unsuccessful. This left most families searching for work outside the community until Joel's business took off.

"Even if I stay, I'll be all but useless for the indefinite future."

"You can't let that happen, Joel. Too many people are depending on you."

Joel jutted both hands out, palms up. "I don't know what you want from me, Daed. There's no other Amish community nearby, and ours has eight families, none of which seem equipped to give the help I need."

"Marry her."

"What?" Joel blinked, unable to grab a clear thought. "Who?" The moment he asked, he knew. "Are you crazy?"

"Maybe. But hear me out. She's here, and she's good with the children."

Daed had detonated another explosive inside Joel's war-torn heart. How could he think clearly enough to have this conversation? Nothing made sense, especially not this craziness. "You just said she can't stay here."

"A single woman cannot stay here alone with you. No matter how innocent your intentions are, we'd be in hot water with the church at large and our families outside of Forest Hill.

They could easily cut off much-needed outside support if they thought Rose's presence in your home to be scandalous."

"So you want me to marry a stranger. I couldn't tell you the color of her hair or the color of her eyes, but I should marry her?"

"Florence was your everything. Do you have a hope of loving anyone like that again?"

Joel's vision blurred with tears. *This* answer he knew. "No."

"Then the only other reason to marry is for the sake of your children, and you have no time to dally in finding someone. Your Mamm has spent time with Rose. There's something about her, something that says she would be willing to—"

"No one is willing to enter a marriage like that, including me."

"Forget what's normal or conventional. Focus on what the children need—your fragile, helpless newborn daughter most of all. Let this second marriage be a sacrifice in honor of what Florence gave you—three healthy children who need far more physical and emotional nurturing than any of us can provide. I've watched Rose for a week, and she's a good caregiver. She's painfully quiet, and she's not comfortable with the womenfolk, but she follows her instincts concerning the children and makes good decisions. I think she's a viable solution. Really, Joel, she's the *only* solution."

Joel sighed. What a mess. "You really think she would consider it?"

"Your Mamm tried talking to her, but like I said, she doesn't respond well to other women. So I talked to her. I asked her directly if she had someone special back home, and she said no. Then I laid out the situation to her. That was a couple of days ago, and I asked her to think about the possibility, you know, if you saw the need for it. She listened and asked a few questions, but she didn't volunteer any thoughts about it one way or the other. I couldn't see putting her on the spot for an answer until you agreed to it." Daed picked up the sugar packets and shook them, causing an irritating rattle. "What you need to do is think of some benefits you and this community can offer her."

"You speak as if it's another business deal we're making."

"That's exactly what it would be, Joel."

What did he have to offer? He knew that deep inside he was broken and couldn't be put back together again. And he had three very young children, which would be a monumental task for the most loving mother, much less a stranger. All he had to offer her were long, hard days of work for children who weren't hers and a life with a man who would never love her. Why would any woman agree to that?

"Son?"

His Daed was waiting for an answer.

Joel nodded. "Ya. If you say it's the only way, I have to trust that." What choice did he have?

Daed stood. "I'll go talk to her now."

"No." Joel was in no condition to make this request, but he had to look her in the eyes as they talked. It would be unfair to Rose if the arrangements were made by someone else, and if he could do only one thing for her, he would treat her fairly and like a partner at all times. "Ask her to come see me."

His Daed left the shop without a lantern and disappeared into the dark night.

Joel covered his mouth with his clasped hands. "Dear God, what am I doing?"

No answer came. He closed his eyes, trying to focus, and it became clear that if Rose agreed to this insanity, he would need to take notes. He got a pen and paper from the designing bench and returned to the barstool. They needed something he could refer back to later, because if the last week was any indication, he would be hard pressed to remember much of what took place tonight.

Ten minutes later Rose tapped on the door and then entered. She stood by the door, looking ready to bolt, a coat on her shoulders and her hands clasped over a dirty black apron. Had she had time to shower or wash her clothes since arriving? For the first time he noted that she was young and that she had reddish-brown hair and freckles on her pale skin. Unlike his Florence, who had black hair and skin that turned golden brown in summer, Rose looked as if she would burn easily and never tan. If she stayed, he would need to remember about her fair skin and not let the summer gardening scorch her. He gestured at the stool closest to him. She eased onto it and rested her hands in her lap.

"How old are you, Rose?"

"Twenty-one."

She was older than she looked, and he was grateful for that.

"And, I'm sorry, your full name?"

"Rose Kurtz."

He wrote that down. "Rose, I . . . I need a mother for my children."

She stared at him with large chestnut-colored eyes, but she didn't respond, not even a nod to acknowledge she'd heard him. He'd read volumes in Florence's eyes over the years, but Rose's gave away nothing.

He rubbed the back of his neck. "Would you be willing to stay here, to live in the house with us?"

Her shoulders moved a bit, and he realized she was wringing her hands together in her lap. She didn't respond. Joel prayed for wisdom.

When five minutes had passed and she still had said nothing, he almost felt as if Florence whispered in his ear. He repeated aloud the question he'd heard. "Are you longing to return home?"

She pursed her lips, looking as if she wasn't going to respond. "No." Her voice was so soft he barely heard her.

"Okay, that answer is good, helpful. We're getting somewhere, right?" They were just doing so very slowly.

Considering what all Amish couples went through in order to marry, this would probably be the shortest courtship on record and would involve no actual courting, romance, or attraction. He and Florence had dated for two years, married when he was twenty-five and she was twenty-four, and conceived their first child on their honeymoon. Life had been one glorious blur since they fell in love. Their glory had burned bright. Now his light and joy was buried in the cold ground, and he was at a messy bench in a workshop, proposing marriage to a stranger. How had four years of marriage gone by so quickly? He imagined that he'd live another forty years and that they would stretch out like an eternity.

Cries from his newborn filled the air, and he looked out the window. A woman draped in a blanket was stepping onto the porch. She went to the porch swing, clearly trying to soothe the infant, but Grace screamed as if in pain. Rose stayed put, but the wails grew louder rather than softer. She got up and ran out of the building without saying a word.

Who behaved so strangely? He watched through the window as she hurried across the lawn and onto the porch. Maybe thirty seconds passed before silence reigned. Whoever she was, he needed her, and he would have to adjust to life with a peculiar woman who seemed to tolerate talking to men only slightly more than talking to women.

They had to finish this conversation, and he wouldn't ask or expect Rose to come to the shop again. He closed the thermos and shoved it into the canvas bag. He did the same with the pad and pen before blowing out the lantern, grabbing the empty mug, and leaving the shop. When he climbed the steps to the porch, his Mamm turned to face him. "I'm sorry for interrupting." She removed the blanket from her shoulders and held it out to him. "Grace's cries upset the boys, and they started crying too, so I brought her out here. But if I'd realized—"

"It's fine, Mamm." He took the blanket. "Just give us time to talk, okay?"

She nodded and went inside. Rose still had her coat draped over her shoulders as she moved to the porch swing. Joel set the canvas bag on the floor. He couldn't make himself sit next to her. It was all he could do to conceal the offense he felt. It should be Florence cuddling their baby, not Rose. Florence would have a tired smile on her lips as she showed him the newborn for the thousandth time, and then she would kiss him on the lips and thank him for loving her. And he would return the words. Warmth and love would fill him anew, adding to his ongoing happiness. If Florence were here, their sons wouldn't burst into tears whenever Grace cried, a reminder of the moment their lives changed.

Rose gazed at Grace. "It would be a noble thing to stay and care for Mose, Levi, and Grace."

"That's true. Maybe the most noble thing I've ever known anyone to do."

She studied Grace, seemingly lost in thought for a very long time, and Joel realized he would have to adjust to sharing a home with a woman who withheld her thoughts from him, leaving him to guess what was going on inside her. Maybe over time it would get better, but right now it was exhausting.

She fidgeted with the baby blanket, never looking up from Grace. "If I agreed to marry you, what would that mean?"

"Fair question." Joel stepped a little closer and leaned against the porch rail while facing the house. "All I'm asking is that you be the children's caregiver—be a good stepmother."

The swing swayed back and forth, but she said nothing. Joel pulled a lighter from his pocket and lit the kerosene lamp on a small half-circle table near her. He pulled the thermos and mug out of the bag, poured coffee, and held it out to her. "I don't have any cream, but would you like some sugar?" He held up a packet of sugar.

She neither took the coffee nor answered his question. "If I stay, I don't want the children yelled at, ridiculed, or spanked."

He set the coffee on the table near the lantern and took the paper and pen out of the bag. "I'll write that down and anything else. Then I'll sign it."

"That's it?" she asked without hesitation. "I ask and you simply agree?"

He leaned against the railing again. "What you're asking is reasonable. I'm in no position to negotiate." He finished writing the sentence and looked up. "What else, Rose?"

She tucked the blanket around Grace's face, caressing the newborn's chin like a nurturing mom. "I like the Englisch woman, the veterinarian, Elise, who is my connection to getting donated breast milk for Grace."

How did that piece of information fit into this conversation? At least it was a hint that she might not be as uncomfortable with all women as his Mamm and Daed said she was with the Amish women who had filled his home last week.

"We've not met . . . that I recall, but I'm glad you like her." Was that what she was looking for—acknowledgment of how she felt? Then, just out of reach of his understanding, he caught a hint of what she might be saying. Again it seemed as if Florence were whispering in his ear, and he said the words aloud. "You would be welcome to build a friendship with her."

Rose sat up a little straighter, and she pointed at the pen and paper, making a circular motion with her index finger. He wrote that down, and a bit of hope began to rise. Elise was important to her. It'd taken forty minutes to squeeze sixty seconds of responses from her, but he now had the feeling that even if his Mamm or Erma were up to keeping the children, Rose would do the best job with them. He wasn't sure why he felt that way, except that he sensed Florence was pulling for him to secure an agreement with Rose.

He tapped on the paper. "What else do you want?"

There was another long pause before she whispered something.

Whatever she'd said, he had a strong feeling it was very important. He put the pen to paper. "Could you repeat that?"

She drew a ragged breath, paused, and finally spoke. "Kindness."

He looked up from the pad. For a faint moment he saw her, a real person. She wasn't an invisible woman or unnoticed servant who had skills he needed to accomplish a task. She had thoughts and opinions that should matter, but he knew they wouldn't, not to a man who was simultaneously numb and in extreme pain from grief. The request for kindness was vague. Did that mean she needed him to speak softly at all times or to do acts of kindness every day? A verse his wife often had quoted came to him. *Be not forgetful to entertain strangers: for thereby some have entertained angels unawares.*

"I will do my best. What else?"

She pulled the baby closer. "A room with a lock."

He set the pad on the railing. "I'll give you the master bedroom." He couldn't stand being in there. It smelled of Florence and lost love. "But you won't need a lock." He moved to the empty space beside her. "If you agree to marry me, we will work together, doing our best to be a good team for the children's sake, but I won't ask that of you. I promise."

Her shoulders slumped as she seemed to relax all over, and a faint smile lifted her lips. "I'm a hard worker."

His eyes misted. He had just acquired the impossible—a full-time, live-in caregiver for his motherless children. A weight lifted from his soul. "I can see that." He hated to push her, but he had to know. "How long do you think it will take to square this plan with your family?"

"We only need to go through the church. Your Daed is a bishop, ya? He needs to talk to Nat, my bishop. That's all. After they've talked, if I get on the phone and say it's what I want, Nat will agree to it and inform my family. My family will grumble among themselves, but they won't push back against a man of God."

Amish women were realistic, but Rose took the cake. He was sure that kind of practicality would serve her well in the years to come. "I think we could give your Mamm and Daed time to get here for the ceremony."

"No need."

He studied her. She didn't want her Mamm here to help

with the transition? To hug her and assure her she was doing the right thing? "A visit is bound to help them feel better about where you'll live and—"

"They'll be fine . . . other than missing a set of hands." She held the baby close, watching her. "I don't want to go back, and I don't want you to invite my Mamm here. Not before we're officially wed, when she'll have no more say over my life."

If Rose didn't have a good relationship with her Mamm, and clearly she didn't, had desperation and grief tricked him into thinking she would be a good stepmother to his children? A week of helping others take care of them was very different from being on her own with three little ones—two in diapers and one barely out of them. But Joel needed her, and there wasn't time for second-guessing.

Maybe her not having to return home was the one thing Joel had to offer her. That, kindness, and the right to be friends with that Elise woman. He wondered if she would come to regret making only those simple requests.

3

Three years later

Shafts of light came through the shop windows, making the fine particles of sawdust look a bit like rolling fog. Joel breathed in the thick aroma of cedar as he cut another strip for the hull. He slid the handsaw back and forth, trying to keep each movement smooth despite the hardness of the wood. The handcrafted canoe business couldn't be any better—whether he was in this shop on his property, at the shipping warehouse near the train depot, or working at the small store in Hinton on Bluestone Lake.

Rose was the reason his business hadn't gone under after he lost Florence, and now it flourished, but Rose would never accept any credit for his success. After Florence died, he couldn't think, and he just wanted to sit and stare into the distance. It took him ten hours to do what he'd once done in two. But Rose was a patient and encouraging woman, supporting his efforts no matter how paltry they were. She hadn't been demanding, only determined to help him carry his grief.

The dinner bell clanged four times, pulling him from his thoughts and letting him know that food would be on the table in forty minutes. Rose would ring it twice more before dinner was on the table, because she knew his tendency to lose track of time when working. Actually, she seemed to know everything about him—every fault and strength—but even his worst shortcomings didn't seem to bother her. He finished cutting the long piece and set the strip on his workbench.

His children's laughter caught his attention, and he moved to the open doorway. Fall had arrived, and colorful trees dotted the land. Crisp air hurried here and there while his children played tag in the yard.

"Mama, help." Grace giggled as she ran as fast as her three-year-old legs could go, trying to tag her oldest brother.

Rose hurried out of the house, a kitchen towel draped over one shoulder, a smile beaming brightly as she pointed a finger at Mose. "Oh, think you're fast, huh?" She scooped up Grace and held her face forward and then took off running toward Mose and Levi. All three children chittered with laughter as Grace tried to tag Mose from Rose's arms.

Joel would never understand why Florence had to die so young, but he was grateful every day that God, in His mercy, had brought Rose to them. Despite Rose's abusive childhood, she was thoughtful and kind. Still, he knew that parts of her were shattered and fragmented. They'd talked about it, and even though she hid the pain and distorted thinking from that trauma as much as possible, they manifested themselves, mostly in her inability to allow any emotion that wasn't positive.

They had both talked at length about their pasts. Other than Florence, no one had ever known him as well as Rose did. But her insecurities ran deep, and she often thought he was angry or displeased with her, even when he told her the opposite. *That* was her Achilles heel. She was unable to accept any praise as heartfelt or to believe she was worthy of being loved.

He hoped to be the same blessing to her that she was to him and his children, but he had to walk lightly. Although she could talk about the sadness and pain of her past, when present events made her sad or angry or hurt her, she withdrew without telling him why. He simply had to accept the wall she put up between them. In the home where she'd grown up, apparently any negative emotion was forbidden, so she'd spent more than two decades burying, hiding, and fearing those feelings. Maybe one day when something hurt her or angered her, she would finally trust him enough to let him see it. That's what he prayed for.

Grace reached down again from Rose's arms and tagged

Mose. He tried to tag Grace again right away, but Rose turned her back to him, put Grace's feet on the ground, and sent her running for base while blocking Mose from reaching her.

Joel chuckled, taking in the antics as if they were a show.

He did love Rose. How could he not? She had saved him from himself and saved his children from being motherless. Still, the journey to this point hadn't been an easy one.

When they began their marriage, it'd been awkward and uncomfortable. Having a complete stranger become a lifetime housemate had been far more daunting than it probably sounded to others. His and Rose's idiosyncrasies were enough to be constant sources of stress. Unlike couples who had fallen in love and wanted to marry, they couldn't rely on fond memories or recall the good qualities that had drawn them to each other, because there were none. They'd had no choice but to learn quickly to accept each other in a peaceful manner. They'd had to trust each other, even though neither had earned it. They'd had to learn how to work together because parenting three children under five demanded skilled and patient teamwork.

The first year they were married, Joel had been so grief stricken he hardly talked. But they inched through the uneasiness of being strangers, and despite his dysfunction and long work hours, somehow they became stable partners, and he learned to breathe again.

The question on his mind of late was how could he show his love if she couldn't accept it. There had to be a way.

One thing he did know—Rose had nothing to call her own, no private joy that wasn't connected to serving him and his children. She slept in his and Florence's former bedroom. She lived in Florence's former home and raised Florence's children. Joel longed to give her at least one thing that she would enjoy that was all hers. But getting her to do something, such as a hobby, for the sheer joy of it would be a tough sell. He might have a better chance of selling canoes in a desert.

With Mose now chasing his younger brother, Levi, while Grace clapped, Rose moved to the clothes hanging on the line. The sun bore down, and she didn't have on her broad-brimmed hat. He removed his straw hat and strode toward her.

She walked down the line, feeling various garments, removing some and leaving others. She spotted him and smiled.

"Hi." He set his hat on her head. "Bright sun, no humidity. You'll burn quickly."

Did she know how much he enjoyed her company?

"Denki." She nodded and passed him the few dry items she'd removed from the line. "How goes the canoe building?"

He held out his arms like a forklift, waiting for her to add more clothes. "Good. I took your idea about using four strips of all dark wood at the bow."

"Does it look good?"

"Very. Care to see it?"

"Absolutely." She jerked the clothes from his arms, walked to the basket, and tossed them in. She turned toward the children. "Don't run toward the road. Got it?"

Mose paused, saluted, and took off in the opposite direction from the road.

Joel and Rose walked toward the shop.

Three years ago, in the first week of November, when Grace was barely a month old, Rose had planned a camping trip. He'd thought she was nuts, but she said she had always wanted to camp and ignored him as she continued to pack camping equipment and food.

Despite her insecurities she trusted her gut about certain things—like getting milk for Grace by finding Elise, who had La Leche experience—because she believed that God was giving her instructions and that ignoring them would be disobedient. But he hadn't known those things about her then. When everything was in the rig for the camping trip, she put his children in too, little Grace in an infant seat, secured to the carriage bench with leather straps. Rose was determined to go, and he could join them or stay home.

Frustrated and concerned about her judgment, he had no choice but to go with her, so he climbed in. She drove about five miles to a campsite, and he helped her set up. After dinner and s'mores around a campfire, Rose took Grace and two-year-old Levi home with her for the night. Joel was left there with a very excited three-year-old. The next morning when Joel woke, he understood why Rose had pushed him to go camping. He'd slept. Something about the fresh air and not being inside the home he'd shared with Florence allowed him finally to sleep more than an hour before bolting awake. It was the first of many regular camping trips Rose planned. After a year of camping when time allowed, Rose and the two younger ones began staying the night, the girls in one tent and the boys in another. He discovered that he, Rose, and the children loved camping.

In her quiet, funny, imperfect ways, Rose spent two years beckoning him to join life again, to soak in the joy and milestones of his growing children, to once again taste the food he put in his mouth, to appreciate each season—snowfalls and skating on icy ponds, summertime campfires and fishing in the creek, and long hikes in the fall.

Friendship, respect, and family made life worth living. But beyond those things, she was odd. A loner who liked super-organized closets, drawers, and cabinets but would make forts out of the living room furniture and enjoy the children's messy playroom.

They went into the workshop, and she walked over to the canoe that he'd almost completed rather than the one he was sawing strips for. Her hands slid over his work, and pleasure filled her face. "Joel, it's perfect and beautiful." She walked around it, her fingers gliding across the gunwale until she was near him again. "It's as if each canoe is more stunning than the one before."

"Denki. Most of the intricacies of the special designs were your ideas. Maybe you should try your hand at building one."

She laughed and held up one arm, poking her biceps. "I'd never get one piece of wood sawed."

"I could do that part. We could build one together. I think you'd enjoy doing something different, something other than housework and taking care of the children."

She shook her head, and he saw insecurity creep into her features. "I'd only slow you down, and nothing we made would compare to what you do on your own. My only skill outside of the home is kennel cleanup."

The answer to his question smacked him in the face. Why hadn't he realized this before? Elise had a kennel on her property, and when Rose visited her, they often spent time in the kennel. Rose always enjoyed her time with the veterinarian and came home gushing about the dogs—old ones as well as puppies.

"Okay, kennel it is."

Rose stopped admiring the canoe and looked up. "Pardon?"

"I want you to pick one day a week and spend the whole

day at the kennel. Mose will be in school, and Mamm can keep Levi and Grace."

"You don't even like Elise."

"That's not true. I do like her."

Rose raised a single brow, questioning his statement.

"Okay, you're right. I don't enjoy her personality that much, but because you like her, I like her." It had taken him some time to figure out what it was about Elise that Rose liked. The woman had strong opinions about everything—from when the children needed new shoelaces to what Rose should feed them for breakfast—and she shared them all the time. She was well educated and seemed to think she knew more than Rose about everything, and he didn't like that. But then he realized that Elise's outspoken ways somehow helped Rose connect with the thoughts and feelings she repressed. Rose often disagreed with Elise's opinions, but hearing Elise's ideas seemed to help Rose sort through her own thoughts on the matter. She truly enjoyed it.

Joel shuffled forward until he was toe-to-toe with his wife. "Would you do this for me? I take and take, and I want to give you something all your own. Go to the kennel one day a week. Enjoy it as a hobby."

"That's nonsense. I won't spend good work time on a hobby."

He removed his hat from her head, revealing her reddish-brown hair that was partly covered by her prayer *Kapp*. "Please."

She studied him. "But . . ."

"I'll help you with the house."

"You do that already."

"I can hire help then."

"Joel, stop."

He tempered his frustrations. "Would you submit to my desire in this as your husband?"

She lowered her chin, looking chastened, but nodded. "Of course."

He hated to push that on her, but if she'd begin going, she would be pleased he'd done so. "Rose, it's only one day a week, and it would be something you would enjoy."

"I can hardly get laundry done each week. How could I commit to every week?"

"Okay, you're exempt when unavoidable things come up."

She seemed leery but nodded again.

"Ya?" He grinned, pleased to finally get her to agree to do something that was just for her. And it'd only taken three years.

One year later

The crisp smells of December filled the air as Rose stood near the driveway, scrubbing clothes on a washboard. She doused her husband's white Sunday shirt with more detergent and rubbed the stains against the washboard. Her stinging hands inspired her to think a series of colorful but unspoken insults about the wringer washer that was sitting in the house, refusing to work.

"Mama!" Levi yelled. "Look."

She grinned. "Ya, that's good."

Since they'd lost their Mamm, Rose had come up with a name the children could call her that felt very mom-like without using the name Florence had gone by.

"No, Mama. Really look," Levi yelled.

Still scrubbing the stains, Rose looked up. Levi hopped off his scooter, spun it around, and jumped back on it. At six years old, he still wanted her attention and approval. She hoped to hold on to his sweet innocence for as long as possible.

"Now I've seen you do it twice," she teased.

All three children were on scooters, riding in circles on the driveway. The boys were on two-wheelers, speedily going into the grass and then back to the top of the asphalt driveway, but four-year-old Grace had a three-wheel scooter, and she liked the smooth and easy ride of the driveway.

Clarabelle mooed softly from her stall. As much pet as milk provider, she probably wanted to come out and play with the children.

Mose sped past Rose, splashing through the watery mess. Maybe she should've set up her wash on the driveway rather than beside it. The ground under and around her was now a muddy mess after hours of water trickling from the wash and rinse tubs. She'd created a mudhole without meaning to.

Looking into the dark puddle, she worried that it served as a reflection of the thoughts that kept bubbling up. She'd been positive she could ignore the dull ache inside her chest. And the unfamiliar jealousy that warred inside her. And the sadness at her husband's waning interest.

She drew a breath and looked up, hoping to find some solace. The trees on her beloved rolling hills of West Virginia were stripped. The colorful fall foliage with its gorgeous shades of yellow and red was gone, whisked away by autumn's winds and pelting rain. But there was equal beauty in the bareness. Some years the land was covered in a thick layer of white by this time, and since Christmas was only six days away, the landscape would surely glisten with its first snowfall soon.

He had found her attractive for a while, hadn't he? Not so very long ago she'd thought they were heading in the right direction—the less lonely direction.

Yesterday Rose had heard the preacher say "nothing lasts forever." In her mind it evolved into *It won't last forever.* The words kept playing in her head last night, getting louder as her house got quieter. What was the *it* that wouldn't last forever? Her loneliness? Her hopes? Those same words—*it won't last forever*—were still with her when she went to bed. But while it was still dark, she awoke suddenly. She checked the ticking clock on her bedside table: 5:20. And then she heard a woman's voice. Rose had darted out of bed to look out the window, her heart in her throat. In the moonlit darkness she saw her husband and Gertie Mae Yoder leaning against the side of the new addition to the house as they talked. What was she doing here?

Rose and Joel were married! Okay, so it wasn't a love-story union, but still, they had stood in the living room with his children in their arms and promised faithfulness and kindness to each other. She didn't know much, but she knew it wasn't a kindness to be chatting with a widow in the wee hours of the morning while your wife slept a story above you.

She continued to scour his shirt, scraping it against the washboard like the angry woman she was. Could fear and frustration turn her into a bitter shrew, like Florence's Mamm? Joel had remarked how cheery Erma was before losing her daughter, how positive despite chronic pain. Now she was a thorn in everyone's flesh. Rose didn't want to be that person; she couldn't imagine it. What would Joel think of her if she turned into an old nag?

But how was she supposed to feel about seeing him with Gertie? Did the woman have special charms, other than being closer to his age, a widow who understood his situation, and absolutely beautiful?

The moment Gertie had arrived in Forest Hill six weeks ago, Rose overheard Erma say how much the woman looked like Joel's Florence, with her delicate features, dark hair, and bronze skin. She'd moved here from Lancaster, where Florence's family hailed from, and Joel used to visit the town with his wife. Gertie had children—two boys and two girls. So he and Gertie had all sorts of things to talk about. She was currently living with an aunt and uncle and trying to raise laying hens and start an egg business. Rose imagined throwing a dozen of

Gertie's eggs against the workshop wall and then felt a rush of heat in her cheeks. What was she thinking?

She wiped the back of her wrist across her brow, where tiny wisps of hair made her flushed face itch. She studied the addition to the house. What was Joel trying to accomplish? The room was on the first floor of the house, right off the kitchen. It was far away from her current room, which was on the second floor, across from the children's bedrooms and just down the hallway from where Joel slept.

He hadn't mentioned building the new room until he was just days away from beginning the work, and he said something that led her to believe he was adding a second dining room, a good space for having Sunday meetings without needing to move furniture out of the house. Two weeks later he'd cut an opening in the side of house, poured the foundation, completed the rough framing, and worked fast to put up interior walls connecting the new room to the existing home. About that time he casually mentioned it would be a bedroom for her.

Why? *Nanny's quarters,* her dark thoughts murmured. To keep her separate from the family now that the children slept through most nights.

When she learned it was for her, she'd been too bitterly disappointed to keep her feelings inside. She wasn't going to let him separate her from the children or make it easier for him to visit with Gertie at any hour of the day, so with tears streaming down her face, she flat-out told him she wouldn't ever move into it. That was two weeks ago, and when he learned how she felt, he put up the beautiful set of double doors that had been delivered a day earlier, closed them, and hadn't worked on the room again.

Good grief. Rose was desperate to talk to Elise. If the washer hadn't broken down, Rose would've spent half the day helping Elise do whatever was on her to-do list while they talked. Elise had opinions galore and no fear of sharing them. Rose often couldn't take her advice, but she liked hearing her take on things.

Mose brought his scooter to a stop in front of her and sniffed the air. "Is dinner on?"

At seven years old Mose was capable of eating almost as much as his Daed, sometimes more. She was never sure if Mose ate too much or if Joel ate that little. Neither father nor son had any extra weight.

"Look at this face." Rose pointed at herself. "Would I forget something as important to you as a full meal?"

"It's been a bad day. You said so."

That it had, starting with what she'd seen before daylight.

When he'd arrived home from school and she didn't have a snack waiting for him, she'd told him that a few things had knocked her off schedule. Fortunately, it took only ten minutes to mix a batch of his favorites, no bakes. "Food comes ahead of clean laundry, right?"

He smiled, nodding his head. "I can wear dirty stuff. I can't eat what isn't there. So when will it be ready?"

"When your Daed comes home from work." She would serve him a nice dinner and sit in her place beside him, but she wondered what would happen if she dumped the food into his lap.

Mose rubbed his nose, the wheels in his head clearly turning. "How do you know it won't be done before then?"

This was a dinner ritual—Mose questioning everything she knew about cooking. "Because I planned on it being ready at five thirty."

"But there's no clock out here."

"True." She sniffed the air. "But I don't smell anything burning. Do you?"

Mose's eyebrows knit. He took life seriously, and Rose tried to help him find humor whenever possible.

In his childlike way of pondering his great worry, Mose put both feet on the scooter and balanced on it. "If we can smell smoke, it's already burned."

"Then we'll know it's done, right?"

He studied her, a slow smile causing adorable dimples. "You're funny."

"I try." She dipped the freshly scrubbed shirt into a vat of clean water. In the boy's defense, she'd burned more than one dinner over the last four years.

"Is your mama funny too?"

"Not exactly." That was an understatement, but over the last four years, she and her Mamm had worked toward a decent relationship, one that existed mostly through writing letters four or five times a year. And she talked to her Mamm, Daed, and brothers every Christmas Eve. It wasn't much, but it's all her family seemed capable of.

Mose continued standing there as if she had a better answer for him.

"You should go before I make you wash the clothes while I ride the scooter."

He abandoned his questions and returned to riding up and down the driveway with the other two.

About a month after she and Joel were married, she wrote to her Mamm. She asked Joel to read it, to make sure she'd been respectful. He'd said her kindness toward her Mamm moved him deeply, so she sent it. A week later her Mamm wrote back, but the letter was filled with anger, even mentioning mistakes Rose had made while doing chores as far back as when she was nine. When Joel read it, he wrote the next letter to Mamm, stating that her response was unacceptable and that she wasn't to write to Rose again unless she was kind.

A year later Rose's Mamm wrote again, this time without

listing any grievances against Rose. Joel's intervention, his firm but gentle hand with her Mamm, was the only reason she and her Mamm had any contact at all.

Rose broke free of her thoughts. Her hands were stiff and wrinkled from the now-frigid water. She imagined her fingers cracking into little pieces, but she wouldn't stop scrubbing. If it would make any difference between Joel and her, she'd scrub the clothing until her flesh had become a part of the fabric.

"Mama!" Grace's panicked voice grabbed Rose's full attention. She glanced in every direction and then realized her girl's voice had come from the barn.

When had she gone in there? The boys were at the edge of the grass, so they weren't beside their sister to help with whatever was happening. Rose took a step in that direction, but her apron caught on the broken metal handle of the washtub.

"Mama! Help!" Grace's scream pierced Rose's heart.

"Let go!" Rose yelled at the tub while jerking her apron free. The tub fell over, dumping clean white shirts onto the muddy ground. Ignoring it, she ran as fast as she could. "I'm coming, baby. I'm coming!" She ran into the barn, the two boys close behind her.

The neighbor's rooster, Hank, flapped around the barn, wings spread as he chased Grace. If Rose had a gun, she'd shoot it and have it for dinner! She got between the old bird and Grace and grabbed her. "Up the ladder. All of you." She lifted

Grace as high as she could, setting her feet on the fifth or sixth rung. "Go on."

Grace was crying as she climbed toward the loft, and Rose feared Hank had drawn blood, but right now she had to distract it while the boys climbed up too. This had to be the meanest rooster that ever lived. Once the children were in the loft, she scurried up also. "Grace, are you hurt?"

"Mama." Grace buried her body against Rose, sobbing.

"Shh, sweetie, it's okay." While soothing Grace, Rose inspected her arms and legs and didn't see any scratches. "Your face, baby. Let me see your face and eyes."

Grace tilted her head back, holding her misty eyes open wide. Rose drew a sigh of relief and rocked her until she was peaceful again. Hank stayed in the barn, pacing back and forth, but he seemed disinterested in hopping and flying up to the loft. The old bird was too decrepit to get up high like the young ones could.

Rose set Grace to the side and kissed the top of her head. "Wait here. I'll show that rooster who's boss."

"Nee!" All three children screamed.

"I'm fine. Watch." Rose swung her feet onto the ladder. "And I'll teach you a thing or two you can use when you're just a little bit bigger."

Grace grabbed Rose's wrist. "Please, Mama, no."

The boys' faces showed sheer distress. Should she cave and do as they wanted or go down the ladder and do what she needed to do—run Hank off? Knowing what to do as a parent never came easy. Indulging the children wouldn't teach them how to overcome, but if she left them now, would it traumatize them, making them more afraid of roosters rather than less?

She looked into the sweet, earnest eyes of her little ones and sat back down in the loft. "Okay." Rose waggled her shoulders and held out her fist. "Who's up for a game of rock, paper, scissors?"

By Amish tradition Grace should be spoken to only in Pennsylvania Dutch, and she should speak only that language until she started school in two years. But Rose didn't think that was helpful. She wanted all three children to excel in learning, and getting a head start on the English language seemed wise. This way when they went to museums in Charleston or Charlottesville with Elise and her girls, Rose's children at least understood the language if not all the history, art, nature, or science principles being shared. The community wasn't thrilled with the way Rose handled certain things, especially going to museums and historical sites, but Joel backed her without fail.

Grace climbed into Rose's lap and tightly wrapped her arms around her mama's neck. Mose and Levi were always ready to try to beat her at any game. They sat on each side of her, but Grace held on tight. Rose and the boys tapped the flat of their fists on their palms two times before revealing their choices. She made the scissors sign.

Levi clapped. "I won! I won!"

Mose shifted, looking more focused. "Let's try again."

Grace released Rose's neck and turned around, watching the game from the safety of Rose's lap. Once Grace felt safe, Rose would go down the ladder and chase Hank away, but right now restoring Grace's sense of safety and the boys' sense of fun was more important.

Grace gasped. "Mama, you're bleeding."

"Am I?" Rose searched for the source of blood and found a gash in her forearm the size of the first joint of a pinkie finger. How had she done that? "Just a little scratch." But it was dripping blood.

Levi pulled a blue cowboy handkerchief from his pocket. He untied it and relieved it of four rocks, two marbles, and one bottle cap. "Here you go, Mama." Levi was the most like his Daed—always ready to help her out of a self-inflicted situation.

"Denki." She put it around her forearm, and Mose tied it. "Denki," she repeated and put her fist in the palm of her hand. "Ready?"

The boys glanced at each other and giggled. "Ready!"

She hoped the rooster would abandon the barn and go home, but whenever they peered over the edge of the loft, he flew at the ladder. "New game time," she said. "Let's do slap hands, but be as easy as you can."

Both boys vied to get in front of her so she would play with them, but she felt Grace wiggling away from her. Grace loved this game, and soon the dark-haired, blue-eyed girl was sitting in front of her with both her hands held out, palms down. Rose put her palms against Grace's, pulled her hands free, and touched the back of Grace's hands. The little girl giggled as if she'd won. The boys played with each other, and a frenzy of hand movements began. Every time a hand was slapped, a burst of giggles came from one of the children. Rose soaked in the sound of their laughter echoing off the rafters.

"Rose?" Joel's voice boomed, and Rose jolted.

"In the barn," she yelled.

Joel's shadow loomed large against the dirt floor before he entered the barn. Hank puffed out his chest and ran at Joel, his wings flapping. Joel kicked dirt at him, making the bird back off, and then grabbed a pitchfork and chased it out of the barn, yelling for it to go home. The rooster disappeared.

Joel turned and looked up at the loft, anger etched across his brow. "Rose." It was the same voice he used when he was disappointed with the children. "Seriously?" He sighed and motioned to the boys. *"Kumm."*

They scurried down the ladder. Rose carried Grace down several rungs before Joel reached up and took her.

Grace hugged her Daed. "You saved us!"

Rose finished climbing down the ladder.

Joel noticed the handkerchief wrapped around her arm. Some of the anger drained from his face. "What happened?"

"I—" She smelled something burning. "Oh, no! Dinner!" She ran out of the barn and across the yard. Joel's best Sunday shirts were lying in the mud puddle, but she kept going. She'd never get those stains out. Once in the kitchen she opened the oven, and smoke rolled out. Her meatloaf and potato dinner wasn't salvageable. She lifted the roasting pan out of the oven, took it to the side of the house, and tossed the burned contents toward the garden. When she turned around, the children and Joel were behind her. Joel stared at the blackened meatloaf. "Hey, guys, can you give us a moment? I need to talk to your stepmom."

The word *stepmom* cut deeper than anything else he could say to her. If he knew how bad that word hurt her, would he still use it? But it would be wrong to insist he call her a name that didn't feel right to him. At least he didn't use it often.

As the children left, Mose looked back, and she saw disappointment on his face. She'd burned his dinner.

Joel stepped forward. "I'll ask again. What happened?"

"The washer broke this morning before I got the first load done, and you'll need the shirts soon, so I improvised, wanting to get the stains out of your best white shirts. While I was doing that, the rooster cornered Grace in the barn, and then the boys followed." She felt like such a child, having to explain what had gone wrong and why.

Joel sighed. "Rose, you can't let something as simple as an ornery rooster rule your day. Why didn't you hitch your rig and go to Elise's house and use her washer?"

She turned away from him. "That wouldn't be right with your Daed being the bishop. And Hank didn't ruin everything. I was making the best of the washer situation, and we were enjoying a beautiful winter day until—"

"Next time kick it or kill it. But don't let it chase the children."

Was he listening? She stopped it from chasing them and got them to safety. *But what about me? Are you concerned for me?* She coached herself to say that out loud, but the words refused to form in her mouth.

Joel turned away from her and gestured toward the upside-down tub and the shirts in the mud. "That rooster," he mumbled and walked toward the washtub.

The conversation was over. She knew it as surely as she knew dinner was burned and her husband would once again sleep on the couch in his small office turned bedroom.

Tears welled, and the darkness of seclusion threatened to

swallow her right there in broad daylight. She wiped her eyes and swallowed hard. She'd made her decision to marry a man who didn't love her.

Mose opened the door and peeked out at her, and through the window she saw Levi and Grace looking at her too. Grace waved and blew her kisses.

Rose drew a deep breath. There were children to feed and kiss and to read to until they all fell asleep.

Joel stood at the washtub. He picked up a muddy shirt, holding it out as if it stank. They'd had a couple of good years, some fun times and laughter, but she never knew what he really felt. He was forced to marry her for the children's sake. It was impossible to forget that.

She pushed the hurt down deep and headed for the house. She had three hungry children to tend to.

Joel set the washtub upright and dropped the muddy shirts into it. "Great," he mumbled. He'd been having a bad day too, one in which clients and shipping contractors had yelled, and it became apparent that he'd made a costly mistake a few days ago.

He'd spent the last few hours simply wanting to come home, help get supper on the table, and tell Rose about his day. Time with her caused his stress to melt, but it seemed as if he often added weight to her days. This wasn't what she needed so close to Christmas—to find time to sew at least one, maybe two, new shirts. He glanced behind him. Rose's shoulders were slumped as she slowly disappeared into the house.

When he was twenty-five, he married Florence, a decision he made of his own free will, and he'd been energized by their love. When Rose had turned twenty-five this past August, she'd been tending to three small children for four years without the free will to leave or choose the life she wanted. She'd complied with his request to marry him because she was unhappy with her family.

He used to be awed at how she maintained her high spirits, but lately he worried that she was too weary and caught in a life she couldn't get free of. In spite of his best efforts, he managed to do little to control the chaos or the work load.

Fire ran through his veins. A year ago Rose had agreed to carve out time to spend one day a week at the kennel, but she hardly ever managed to get away for more than a couple of hours once a month.

One thing he could control was that stupid rooster. He spotted it returning to his barn, and he strode in that direction. Hank screeched and flapped his wings, but Joel cornered him and jerked the bird up by his legs. He squawked, beat his wings, and clawed at him. Joel considered killing Hank then and there. That would solve the problem. But Rose liked the rooster's owners, elderly Englisch neighbors that she bought eggs from. So he walked to the road and went toward the Wagners' place. The rooster flapped and pecked and spurred his hands until they were bloody, but Joel ignored it as best he could. He looked at his dusty work boots and focused on putting one foot in front of the other on the gravel road.

What was happening between Rose and him? They'd come so far, only to have lost their ability to communicate. She stiffened at his presence, refused to hold his hand during the family mealtime prayer, and had stopped meeting him in the living room after the children went to sleep. That's when they used to talk or read or stare at the fire.

Why had things changed?

He wondered if she'd finally realized what she'd given up to marry a man she didn't love. Did she blame him for trapping her in a lifelong relationship? Maybe she was weary of the work load. Whatever it was, he missed her, and while he wanted to be straightforward with her about his feelings, he never was certain how she would react to such boldness.

Before grabbing the rooster and walking off, he should've smiled at Rose and assured her that he wasn't angry or disappointed about the shirts, supper, or anything else. The only thing he'd been upset about was Hank's intrusion and how it had stolen time from Rose's day while adding to her tasks. If that wasn't enough, the rooster had also frightened the children.

The bird kept thrashing and digging its spurs into Joel's hand. He should've grabbed a pair of gloves before capturing Hank, but he'd been too frustrated to think about it at the time.

Joel looked up. George and Shirley Wagner's old faded-gray house with peeling paint and a tin roof stared back at him.

They were good people, but they were forgetful, maybe because of their age. The porch was a catawampus, splintered wreck of half-rotten lumber. He and Rose had offered to fix it, but George wasn't interested.

When Joel put his weight on the first step, it groaned under the pressure. By the time he reached the porch, George was at the front door. Between Hank's complaining and the boards shrieking, Joel didn't need to knock to get the old man's attention. George had on a thick flannel shirt and loose-fitting jeans that were hiked up to his waist by a pair of suspenders.

He looked at the rooster in Joel's hand. "My goodness. You're bleeding."

Joel ignored the remark. "Do you want to keep this bird?"

"Drop Hank and come inside, Joel." George looked over his shoulder. "Shirley! Get a first-aid kit."

"Thanks, but I don't need first aid." Joel tried to keep his voice even, but with each word his pulse quickened. "You aren't listening to me, George."

The old man's thick gray brows furrowed. "About?"

"This." He held up the rooster and wasn't letting go until Hank was inside a fence. "Rose had to usher the children into the loft to keep them safe. You've been good neighbors for a lot of years, but this rooster has gotten mean in his old age. The next time he steps on my property, I'm going to have to kill him."

George stepped back from the door, reached for something, and returned with a pair of work gloves. He slipped them on and took Hank from Joel. "It's a rooster, Joel, not a rabid dog."

"Nonetheless, I've spoken my piece about him. Keep him inside the chicken-wire fence, or be ready to part with him." He hated this conversation. Rose and Shirley Wagner went berry picking together from time to time, and once a year they made jams. But this rooster thing had gone on for far too long.

George nodded. "If the bird enters your property again, I'll kill it myself." The old man attempted a smile.

Shirley came out of the house. "Joel!" She had a tin first-aid kit in her hand. "What happened?"

"Hank got out," George said.

Shirley grimaced, looking appalled and apologetic. "I told you that bird was trouble," she mumbled while opening the kit. "Honest, Joel, we've had our share of roosters over the years, but I've never seen one this mean."

Her reaction diffused Joel's anger. His unchecked words had gotten the better of him again. "It's all right, really."

Shirley retrieved Band-Aids from the first-aid kit.

Joel moved toward the steps. "No, I'm fine, Shirley, really."

He needed to get home. With Christmas approaching and many events this week, Rose could use help getting her day back on track. Stupid washer. It had to break today of all days. He should've replaced it years ago, and now it could take three or four weeks to get one shipped here. They didn't stock wringer washers in the nearest Lowe's.

He was halfway down the porch stairs when Shirley called to him. "Joel, please, it'll only take a second."

"I appreciate it, Shirley, I do. But it looks worse than it is." He was far more concerned with Rose's injuries. She wasn't a complainer, and if anger hadn't gotten the best of him, he would've thought to look after her before jerking up the rooster and walking off.

He continued walking away. Shirley's voice faded, and again he focused on the gravel road. The wind stung his face, and darkness pressed in.

The clomping of hoofs behind him echoed, and carriage wheels crunched against the gravel. The rig slowed and came up beside Joel.

"You need a ride," Erma said over the scraping of hoofs against the road.

His former mother-in-law was the last person Joel wanted to deal with right now. But it was a good sign that she was out and about. Her rheumatoid arthritis often kept her inside, sometimes in bed, for most of the winter. "Denki, Erma, but I'm fine walking." If she gave him a lift home, she would likely decide to go inside to visit, and it wasn't the night for that.

"Oh, don't be silly." She stopped the rig. "Get in."

Joel slowly released a sigh, trying to hide his displeasure as he got into her rig. "You look healthy."

"I've been worse." Erma tapped the reins against the horse's back. "What about you? You're bleeding."

"Ya, just a little."

He really didn't want to explain to anyone and especially not to Erma. If anything went wrong—one of the children had a cold or a scraped knee or seemed overly hungry during the after-service mealtime—Erma complained to or about Rose. It wasn't as if he could tell her to leave his wife alone. Even if his words were gentle, they would only stir up more strife, not put it to rest. Thankfully, Rose usually let Erma's increasingly bitter words roll off, even when she nitpicked at church gatherings in front of others. He ran interference as best he could, and he'd spoken to Erma about her harsh ways, but controlling her was like trying to control Hank.

If Erma's words stung Rose deeply or angered her, she became very quiet and withdrew inside herself. She was skilled at shaking off negative feelings, but when Joel realized what was happening, he would do a little something special for her—make her breakfast or a cup of tea or put up an extra shelf in her closet. His ounce of kindness would pull her out of the hurt or anger, and she would be back to herself in no time. She was a resilient, even-keeled person by nature. But like Hank, Erma could dash out of hiding and stir up trouble while drawing blood.

Joel shifted in his seat. "So what are you doing up this way?"

Erma shrugged. "Took a pie to the Yoders. It's Mary's birthday."

Was that alcohol on her breath? Again? For years she'd said a few sips of rum did wonders for her arthritic pain. She even had a medical report of some kind that supported her claim, so the church leaders had given their permission. But whether the rum was medicinal or not, she shouldn't be on the road if she was under the influence.

He held out his hands for the reins. "You shouldn't be driving."

She glanced his way. "It's a buggy, not a tractor. The horse can do its job with no guidance from me."

So she was drunk and she knew it.

"What clawed you?" Erma asked.

"The Wagners' rooster."

"Those people. Rose should be more faithful to the Amish than to any Englisch neighbors. If she was, she'd buy her eggs from our community."

"We know how you feel, Erma. It's Rose's decision." Joel knew she was alluding to Gertie, the Amish widow who was trying to establish an egg business to support her family.

Erma clicked her tongue in protest. "When we get to your place, I want to go in and see the children for a bit."

"This isn't a good time for a visit."

If she would visit with the children without criticizing Rose, he would welcome her. But it never worked that way.

"It'll be fine," Erma said. "I can hardly get around most days, and you'd keep me from visiting my grandbabies on the rare day I can?"

Joel nodded. "Okay, but not for too long. It's been a rough day."

Erma scoffed. "My Florence would count it a privilege to have a cold day of sunshine while she looked after her three beautiful children." Her face hardened, revealing the depth of her pain. "A hard day is lying dead in the ground and leaving three motherless children."

"Your heartache is justified, and I don't mean to sound as if it's not, but you can't blame Rose for Florence's death."

Erma slapped the reins against the horse's back. "Oh, but how perfectly Rose took advantage of the situation. She waltzed into my daughter's life and simply took over. Florence lived in that drafty rental with you for two years. When you finally got the money to build a house, she worked by your side, clearing the land while tending to a baby and being pregnant with your second child. Once you moved into that house, she worked hard with you to help build the shop and manage the staff and business details as your company grew. Every free moment she had was spent working her fingers to the bone, and then she died giving you what you wanted—children to fill your home."

Her condemnation pressed in on him. Florence didn't have to help clear the land. She wanted to, just as she wanted to be a part of his company. What should he have done—refused to let her be part of things she found fulfilling? Wouldn't that make him an overbearing man, one who tried to control his wife rather than support her? Florence was bubbly and outgoing. She looked forward to interacting with their employees and bringing the children into town to see the work there.

"Look, Florence and I were a team. Despite not having the money to do better, we chose to marry, and we knew we'd live in that drafty rental. You and the community knew it too, and no one minded at the time. We did what young married people do—started out simple, worked hard, and saved. She didn't do anything dangerous during our marriage. The doctor assured me that nothing we did caused her hemorrhaging after Grace was born and that we couldn't have prevented it. I've told you this for four years."

The only thing that could've made a difference was where they were when the hemorrhaging began. In that, he had fault. Florence wanted to have her babies at home just as her fore-mothers had, and he agreed with her that it was safe. She'd given birth twice at home, and everything went well. But if she had been in a hospital when Grace was born, he had no doubts she would be alive right now. Joel used to carry unbearably harsh regrets, but with Rose's help he had accepted that no one was at fault and had forgiven himself and moved forward. It'd been a slow process, but he knew that unforgiveness, whether toward others or himself, was like an infection. Left unchecked, it would destroy part of his heart, and he wanted to be as whole as possible for his children.

It was sad that no one had been able to help Erma forgive others and herself. Joel knew that her husband, Leo, tried to find ways to dig her out of her grief, but her bitterness had deep roots.

She turned on the blinker and slowed the rig as she pulled onto his driveway. "For four years I've watched you fall all over yourself being grateful to Rose. Exactly what are you grateful for? An opportunist who wasted no time in being the first single woman to your door? Unlike my Florence, Rose didn't have to earn the right to be with you. She didn't spend years trying to get you to stop working long enough to realize she existed, but my Florence did. You married Rose without question, and if there is some way to make her life easier, you'll stand against the whole community to do it."

Joel had no defense to offer. Her bitterness had twisted all her perceptions, both past and present. As the rig passed the new addition to the house, Joel shoved his disappointment down deep. He'd started the addition when he thought that Rose and he were on a path to sharing the same bedroom. It was to be a gift—a new room for their new life. A room he had never shared with another woman. He knew that would be important to Rose.

"In her four years of being here, Rose has never helped with your business."

Rose was a giver, but her way of contributing avoided the kind of people interaction required by some aspects of his work. If someone needed food or money, she would till an extra plot of ground and tend the crop. Then Joel would deliver the produce to those in need or find a way to sell it and give them the money. If families in crisis needed childcare, Rose would have a brood underfoot and do a great job, even if it went around the clock for a week. But she wanted no part of the adult socialization.

Erma sighed, looking with great interest at the spot where the washtub sat, and parked the rig next to it. Joel hopped out and went to her side of the rig to help her down.

Erma got her footing by holding on tightly to Joel's hand. Then she released it and walked to the tub. She lifted the two muddy white shirts and looked at Joel.

He arched his eyebrows and shrugged his shoulders. "Like I said, it's been a rough day."

"Bad day? Rose is an inept wife and mother. Open your eyes, Joel. God Himself has judged Rose as unfit."

Unfit? What was Erma suggesting now?

She dropped the shirts back into the tub and headed for the house.

He'd never seen the woman this vindictive toward Rose, and he fell into step beside her. "I've asked you to keep the visit pleasant. If you can't manage that, I need you to leave."

Erma stopped short and leaned toward him like a threatening dog. "You will not keep me from my grandchildren."

"I'd prefer not to." That was putting it lightly. A small community divided by strife became a magnet for contention and resentment. Joel knew that God's preference was a peaceful solution. Was that possible with Erma? "But I can and I will put my foot down if necessary."

She stared at him, clearly trying to size up the situation. "We wouldn't be at odds if you had waited a respectable amount of time to remarry after my daughter died. Then Gertie would have been here, and she would be a much better wife for you."

Gertie, the widow who arrived mere weeks ago—that's what had Erma riled? She was overwrought because he hadn't waited four years to marry someone else? He knew the wisest course was to walk away from this crazy conversation, but the questions came out in a flood. "Why do you still feel this way toward Rose? Can you explain it? You do understand that she nurtured Grace—soothed her and fed her—when no one else could do either, right?"

Erma pointed at the house. "Within hours of arriving in Forest Hill, Rose stood inside my daughter's home and took Grace out of my hands!"

Joel had no recollection of that. Is that why Erma left his house and took to her bed—embarrassment and anger? Had her resentment been building since the night Rose arrived? "It wasn't personal, Erma. Even if Rose had been an angel sent straight from heaven, the loss of Florence would have made seeing Rose as a blessing impossible. Rose couldn't prevent anything that happened concerning our need for her. By the mercy of God, Rose and Grace formed a special bond from the start."

"You mean Rose and *you* formed a special bond from the start. You betrayed my Florence before she was cold in the grave."

"It wasn't about me! I don't understand why you can't get that. Rose has nursed those children through dozens of childhood illnesses. Do you know how well she's kept your grandchildren fed, clothed, and prayed for? The fact that you can't find it within yourself to be thankful, if not to her, then to God, should be a clear indication to you that *you* are the problem, not me or Rose."

"You have more gall than anyone I know. It's no wonder

God closed Rose's womb. God knows what you're unwilling to admit—that Rose is unfit as a wife and mother."

Joel's blood ran hot, and he could only see red. "To conceive, to my understanding, requires sharing a bed. I doubt God has any correction for someone as self-sacrificing as Rose."

Erma stood there, studying him. "You've never consummated your wedding vows?"

The intimate truth of his marriage was no one's business, and regret instantly began to bubble inside him. But maybe it would help if she understood the true nature of their arrangement. "No."

It wouldn't benefit anyone for him to tell Erma that he had slowly but surely fallen in love with Rose. How could he not? She loved to love and to give her all. Over the years she had come to know him in ways no one else had. She'd seen him at his weakest and still found good in him.

He understood that love and romance were two very different things. Romance wasn't part of the agreement they'd made, and unless Rose indicated that she wanted to alter what they'd set in place four years ago, he would quietly long for her but would honor the original arrangement.

Rose woke to a quiet, dark home. Snuggled under the quilt, she didn't want to move, knowing the slightest shift would be another reminder of how cold the sheets were around her. Another winter would come and go, and she would wake each morning in a dark, icy room. Spring and summer and fall were easier, the sun arriving earlier and stretching later into the day. Winter nights in Forest Hill—with her husband asleep on a couch in a room down the hall—seemed to go on forever.

She forced her legs out of bed and sat upright. She struck a match, lit the lantern, and took it with her into the bathroom to shower. It would be another awkward morning between Joel and her until he went to work. If possible, the air between them seemed more stifling now than in her first weeks here. She needed to talk to Elise. Not only could she tell Elise anything, but she trusted Elise's opinion. Once Rose dropped the boys off at school, she and Grace would pop by Elise's, hoping she would be home. Joel's Mamm, Sarah, was a good friend too, but as the bishop's wife, she was very busy this time of year. Besides, Rose would never talk to Sarah about such matters.

Last night Erma had brought Joel home in her rig after his trip to the Wagners', but she didn't come in the house. Maybe she had been irritated about the shirts Rose had ruined. Rose never knew whether to be grateful or disappointed when Erma avoided her. The woman reminded her of her own mother, and that alone was enough to strain the relationship.

When Joel walked in from taking the rooster back, he was spent. So they got through another stilted dinner, and Rose refused Joel's help with the dishes, shooing him into the living room with the children. She was certainly capable of washing dishes by herself. But until recently she had loved having his help in any way that he gave it.

She used to treasure the hour or so after they put the children to bed, when they would work on chores together—things she hadn't managed to get done with the children up and Joel at work. The flames in the kerosene lanterns would flicker and dance while they washed and dried dishes or folded, ironed, and put away laundry. Joel wasn't like most men, at least not since she had arrived, and he didn't mind pitching in. More important than the chores they finished, they had used that time to talk, to help scrub away each other's loneliness.

She got out of the shower, dried, dressed, and pulled her hair back into a proper bun before putting on her prayer Kapp.

When she'd arrived four years ago, the Forest Hill community had wanted to welcome her. She could tell that much, and she gave them credit for their hearts being in the right place. But everything about Rose was a reminder of the loss of Florence. Conversations were labored and filled with land mines, causing people to explode into tears when least expected. Everyone in this small community, including Joel, longed for Florence, but at least he had taken the time to work past the chasm. And she knew he'd done so for her sake.

Now the chasm was created by both of them—Rose, unable to ask for what she wanted, and Joel more of a mystery than ever. She picked up the lantern and opened the bathroom door. Was that coffee and bacon she smelled? She wanted to avoid being alone in the kitchen with him this morning. He'd been up and out of the house early for the past month, so what was different about today?

She drew a breath, bracing herself before she went downstairs. When she reached the kitchen, she saw Joel at the counter, making sandwiches. He looked up. "Morning."

"Hi."

He had water simmering on the stove, ready to add the grits

that were sitting on the counter next to the pot. Toast was made and buttered, and there was a plate of fried bacon cooling on the counter as well as a bucket of fresh milk. He'd already milked Clarabelle?

He'd apologized to her last night, saying that he'd overreacted about the rooster and that it'd been a really bad day at work. Joel put two sandwiches into plastic containers and placed them in the lunchpails. He turned down the burner under the boiling pot of water for the grits, leaving it to simmer until closer to when the children would be ready to eat. With breakfast basically done, the cow milked, and lunches made, Rose wasn't sure what to do with herself.

He grabbed a mug and filled it with coffee. "I want to see your arm where the gash is." He placed the percolator back on the stove and held out the mug to her.

"I'm fine." But she didn't want to take the coffee from him. Not this time. She wanted an explanation of why he and Gertie had been talking outside the house before daylight yesterday morning. Except, she didn't want to know. So she took the coffee. It was easier to go along than to try to explain why she was refusing the drink. Knowing the right moves to make in a marriage seemed so tricky. Was theirs the only marriage like that?

"Can I look?" He gestured at her arm.

She shook her head, embarrassed by the memory of the

dumb bird. "I never finished cleaning up the mess with the laundry." She went toward the closet to get her coat.

"Done." He pulled out a chair at the head of the table and gestured to it. "Sit with me."

"Why?"

His brows knit. "Rose, I know you've enjoyed it when we've had time to talk before the day started." He clenched the spindles on the ladder-back chair and waited for her to sit.

Her heart pounded with confusion and jealousy as the image of him laughing with Gertie tried to undo her.

He jiggled the chair, so she sat.

"I won't bite. I promise." He moved to the chair to her right. "Our season is fast approaching, Rose. Christmastime." He eased his fingers over her wrist and gently turned her arm to look at the gouge, but her sleeve covered it. His fingers were warm against her skin as he carefully pushed her sleeve back. He sucked air through his teeth. "Ouch."

She pulled her sleeve down. "It's not a big deal." But when she tried to ease her arm free of his hold, he didn't let go.

Using two fingers, he gently made wide circles on her forearm, inches below the gash. "We'd been married about twelve weeks before our first Christmas together, and I could hardly breathe or eat from the grief, but you made me laugh for the first time since we met. Do you remember?"

When talking to Rose, he usually dated events by when they met or married rather than by Florence's death. Maybe that was less painful for him, or maybe he was trying to honor his relationship with Rose. Joel was probably the most kind and thoughtful man she'd ever known, even during his darkest hours. But what did he mean by "our season"?

"You look unsure." He continued to caress her arm and stared at her limp hand as if it had some magical power. What was going on with him today? "Let me refresh your memory." He smiled as if teasing her. "On Christmas Eve four years ago, you asked me to take you and the boys to the small pond to ice-skate. It was your first real request, other than camping, so I called Mamm and got her to stay with Grace. I was aimless and disconnected, doing one thing and thinking of another. You not only let me grieve as I needed, but you found ways to help me process all that I felt."

"Did I?"

"Sure, you're smart about the human condition, and you know how to help."

She shrugged, but her chest felt weighted with his emotional words.

"So"—he ran his fingers to the center of her palm—"a light snow was falling from the dark sky, and I had a two-year-old strapped to my back and a three-year-old by the hand as I followed you, because I had forgotten there was a pond in that area." He smiled, looking at peace. "You turned around, facing me while walking backward toward the icy pond, and you said, 'Listen, I'm good on my feet. I don't fall. Ever. But I do random gravity checks.' I had no idea what that meant, but you'd no more than gotten the words 'gravity checks' out of your mouth when you fell backward and thudded to the ground. You immediately jumped up, snow flying off your clothes, and yelled, 'Check!' " He laughed. "You said, 'Gravity still works, especially right here,' and you pointed at the path under your feet." He angled his head, studying her. "The cogwheels that were somewhere inside me were misaligned. But at that moment at least one slid into place and connected with another cogwheel, and then the next, until the hundreds of cogwheels began to move. And I breathed again." His eyes bore into hers. "I thought it was time I told you that."

"Denki, Joel." Why couldn't she just tell him how she felt? Surely a kind rejection from him would be easier than living in eternal torment. But for every million thoughts and feelings she had, she managed to share only a dozen. Knowing this about herself didn't help loosen any of her many words, and that only added another layer of frustration. She tugged harder at her arm this time, and he released her. "I should begin sewing you at least one new shirt. Christmas will be here soon, and you won't have a decent shirt for the service or the church gatherings."

Joel sighed. "Words don't come easy for you. I get that." He leaned back, looking pleased. "I like that about you . . . most of the time. But if you were one smidgen as good with words as you are with actions, I wouldn't be so perplexed about how to proceed. But that's okay, because every couple has an area that gives them trouble. So I've decided we need a code between us, either a word or a signal. If you're displeased, you could yell 'offensive!' or 'check!' One simple word. That's all I would need to begin to piece things together."

"A code? If I'm that broken, I deserve to stay that way," she whispered.

"I was beyond that broken, and you never thought I deserved to stay that way. And you're not broken. You listen to me talk, and you have soothing, healing words. You give wise counsel, and we talk for hours about the children or God. We're a team when it comes to this family, community needs, and business ideas. But, ya, you struggle when it comes to your feelings. Some of that is your personality, and some of it is how tough your Mamm was on you. You avoided a lot of punishment by keeping your thoughts to yourself. Maybe it's a habit as much as anything."

This conversation was making her really uncomfortable, and she just wanted to get busy doing something. She went to the sewing supply cabinet and pulled out white material for new dress shirts. But when she unfolded the fabric, she realized she didn't have enough to make even one.

"Rose." Joel was almost whispering in her ear. "What's going on?" She could feel his warm breath against the back of her neck. "I've stayed up a lot the last few nights, roaming the house and the yard, thinking. We've successfully maneuvered around obstacles of every kind in our four years together, so it doesn't make sense that we're tripping over what seems to be nothing."

Wait. He was outside Monday morning, walking and thinking about them? "Up thinking about us? Why?" She couldn't make herself turn to face him.

"Because we're a good thing to think about . . ." From behind her he rested his hands on her shoulders. "Ya?"

"Maybe. I guess." She refolded the material and set it back in place. "Depends, doesn't it?" If he was roaming around trying to figure out how to cope with her, that wouldn't be a good thing.

"I'm trying not to cross a line here, Rose, but you have to talk to me. Whatever is going on between us, I want to fix it. I miss you."

She couldn't budge. Was he telling her the truth? Doubts swirled. Feeling valuable was never easy. Whenever life grew quiet, she could still hear her Mamm's harsh words constantly telling her all she did wrong. "You miss me?"

He chuckled. "Why is that so hard for you to believe?"

"I'm strange and prone to making small disasters."

"Ya, you are. I'm commonplace, maybe even boring, and I need small mishaps to keep life interesting."

He wasn't commonplace or boring. He was smart and the kind of entrepreneur whose innovation kept this Amish community thriving. And so very cute. Elise had told her that he looked like a younger Mark Ruffalo, a well-known actor in the Englisch world. Rose saw a picture of him recently, and, ya, if one took fifteen years off Mr. Ruffalo, that's who Joel looked like—dark curly hair, gentle eyes, sincerest of smiles, and all.

She narrowed her eyes, studying him. She had no idea why squinting made it seem as if one could see something clearer, but she did it anyway. Why would he miss her? She was right here, being her ordinary self. Quietly loving him and thinking he might never love her back.

"Mama," Grace called from the top of the stairs. Rose glanced at the clock. Grace might be ready to get up, but more than likely she just wanted her covers retucked again. Without saying anything else, Rose went upstairs. "Hi, sweetie." Rose picked her up, and Grace wrapped her precious arms around her neck. "You cold?"

"Ya. I like December because it'll be Christmas soon, but I don't like the cold."

"Me neither." Rose took her back to her bed, laid her down, and pulled the quilts over her. She stayed there for a few minutes, brushing back her dark hair and kissing on her sweet face.

Was it possible that Rose and Joel could live like other married couples, ones who shared a bed and had children? When Grace fell back to sleep, Rose hurried down the stairs. She needed to know the ending of Joel's and her story. But where was he? "Joel?" She looked in the living room. Where could he be? A sound from outside drew her to the kitchen window. There he stood, in their driveway, talking with Gertie and holding what looked to be two folded white shirts.

Embarrassment burned through her—embarrassment that she'd actually believed he cared for her, embarrassment that Gertie knew about the shirts and had made sure he had new ones so quickly—before she, his own wife, could make them for him. How had she sewn two shirts this quickly? She must have been making them for her uncle.

But much more important than that, just who did Gertie think she was? Rose was Joel's wife!

Maybe Rose wasn't good at talking about how she felt, but she didn't need words to go out there and run off Gertie Mae Yoder.

Joel saw the front door fly open. Rose hurried out, her burgundy dress a blur as she rushed toward him. Where was her coat? She stopped directly in front of him, her eyes filled with something unfamiliar. Anger?

"Good morning, Rose." Gertie smiled and gestured toward the unfinished addition to the house. "That'll be really nice when it's done."

Rose nodded. "It looks like we'll get snow soon. I'm sure you have egg deliveries to make, so I'd be on my way if I were you."

Gertie blinked. "Oh." She glanced at Joel. "I . . . I guess I should."

His wife had just invited Gertie to leave, and all three of

them knew it. He'd never seen anything like it, certainly not from Rose.

"Denki for the shirts." Joel tried to sound as if there was nothing unusual about what Rose had just said.

"Anytime." Gertie got in her rig.

Rose remained glued in place, saying nothing, and Joel waited. As soon as Gertie pulled out of the driveway, Rose snatched the shirts out of his hands, walked to the mud puddle, and threw them into it.

At least he knew how she felt. She was seething from the disrespect of another woman stepping in when she wasn't asked, but he guessed that Erma had asked Gertie to make the shirts. Still, his wife wasn't hiding her feelings, and that was a victory. He studied the shirts. "Check!" He studied his wife. "Offensive!"

"Is this funny to you?"

"When a man loses four white shirts over the course of two days to a small puddle in his yard, ya, it's a little amusing."

Rose stormed off, and he took a couple of long strides to get in front of her. He turned to face her, blocking her from going any farther. "Okay, not funny, I guess."

She crossed her arms. "How did Gertie even know about the shirts?"

"My guess is that after Erma left here last night, she made a beeline to Gertie's. I'm sorry, Rose. Erma seems bent on doing or saying things to cause trouble. That aside, Gertie's gift could've saved you the time and trouble of having to sew new shirts for me."

Rose pointed at him. "I'm your wife! Me! Like it or not, that's the way it is!"

"I like it fine, and I'm pretty sure Gertie's glad of it as well."

"Stop making jokes, Joel." She gestured toward the unfinished addition. "I saw you and her out here before sunup yesterday, laughing and talking. And you dare tell me that you were outside at night thinking about me? Flirting with her is more like it!"

Guilt flooded him, but it'd seemed completely innocent at the time. And what was this? Was Rose jealous? If so, that would be a good sign . . . maybe.

"Come on, Rose. You know me better than that." He'd been walking around the house when Gertie was cutting through the side yard. "She was on her way back from the Wagners', actually. We practically bumped into each other."

"Give me a break. Why would she be at the Wagners' home that time of day?" Rose's voice held an edge he had never heard before. "Walking, before daylight, in December!"

Frustration began nibbling at him. "It was her aunt's birthday, and she said she wanted to make Mary a special breakfast but needed an ingredient for the cinnamon rolls, and Shirley Wagner left it on the porch for her. I don't know why she didn't take her buggy. Exercise? I probably should've nipped the conversation in the bud and come inside, but I didn't think anything of chatting with her a bit."

"What a story. I don't buy it."

"Good. Don't buy it. Stay angry. I much prefer that to silence. I have a closet full of work shirts and pants. Throw all of them in the mud." He wanted to get to the bottom of what was going on in her head even if he had to walk around in his underwear all winter.

Rose stood on her tiptoes, pointing at him again. "You tell her that if she comes on this property again without an invitation from me, I'll put *her* in the mud!"

The cogwheels inside his brain finally clicked into place. Had Rose pulled away from him about the time Gertie came to Forest Hill? He had watched the widow in church once or twice and hurt for her. He doubted the relatives she'd moved in with understood the kind of pain she was going through. He wondered how she would survive the loss, how much of her would still be alive in five years. "I'm not infatuated with her. Not even a little."

"Maybe not. I don't know." Rose seemed to have a full head of steam, unable to stop her words now. "But you're building that room for some reason. And you started it about the time Gertie and her children showed up. You know I like being on the same floor as the children, and the fact that you want me in that new room, so far from them, is just the type of thing an employer would do to a nanny."

"A nanny?" So Gertie arrived, and he started building a bedroom that would move Rose away from the children's rooms? He never would have drawn that connection. "Nanny," he muttered again. "You wouldn't come up with these ridiculous notions if you'd just talk to me. The room is for us. You and me."

The anger and hurt on her face changed to shock, and then he realized what he'd said. It was too late to take it back. "There's some good news in all this. Apparently your words flow freely when you're angry enough." He took off his coat and put it around her shoulders. "Don't let the new room or what I'm about to say put any more walls between us, okay?"

She nodded. "I'll try."

"I'm in love with you." He pulled the sides of his coat tighter around her. Those were dangerous words, words that could backfire. Her Mamm had belittled her, but Rose told Joel that after a day or a week or a month of cutting Rose down with her sharp tongue, she would tell Rose that she loved her.

At least for the moment, his wife seemed to be taking his words to heart. "Ridiculously so, because right this second, when I should be frustrated because you didn't trust me with your fears, I could list—without pausing—hundreds of reasons why I love you."

She stared at him, clearly trying to absorb a truth she'd been oblivious to. Any relationship that began like theirs was complex. He and Rose had learned to care *about* each other long before they learned to care *for* each other. And caring for each other came way ahead of learning to like each other. Then love followed, the kind of love that made life worth living.

"A room for us?" She seemed completely caught off guard, and he knew the possibility of that space being for them had never crossed her mind. Why didn't he talk to her about it before she started making off-the-mark assumptions?

"Only if you like the idea, but ya. I didn't want to be too bold about it, so I thought I'd make it your room, a place that has belonged to no one else." He looked heavenward, shaking his head for a moment. "I didn't know how you'd respond to a romantic move, so I thought building a room might start the conversation."

"*This* is a conversation."

Was that a hint of humor? The line was one Levi used to say when trying to talk them into letting him do something. Joel would say that he and Rose would have a conversation and tell Levi their answer later. Levi would then say, "*This* is a conversation." From time to time in private and when playing around, Joel and Rose would use the saying.

Snow began to fall, reminding him of Christmas Eve four years ago and how God gave hope in the most trying times.

Hope fell from heaven as quietly and gently as snowflakes. Their first Christmas Eve had a bit of laughter and hope in it, but what would this Christmas hold for them?

He brushed a drop of water off her cheek where a snowflake had melted. He lifted her chin, angling her head one way and then the other as he studied her eyes. "You're messing with me."

She smiled. "I am."

"You're back." He took a deep breath. "And it only took one month, four muddy shirts, and a rooster in a pear tree." He pulled her close and held her. "But that's okay, because I'd give anything for you to know the truth, that I love you."

She tilted her head back, looking up at him. They'd hugged on numerous occasions, one human holding another, keeping the darkness at bay. It usually happened in the evenings after the children were in bed and they'd spent a couple of hours talking. But she'd always given one final squeeze, slipped from his arms, and retreated to her room. This felt very different.

He caressed her cheek. "How do you feel about my declaration?"

"It's what I want, but—"

"Good." He held her face, one thumb caressing her lips. That's all he needed to hear. The rest of her sentence could wait. He lowered his lips to hers, and when she kissed him back, he felt as light as the snowflakes around them. Their kiss grew deeper by the moment, and he could feel her pleasure in it.

She pushed back.

"Wow." He needed a moment to catch his breath. "Where did that come from?"

"I'm . . . not sure . . ." Her frosty breaths were short and quick.

"And the *but*?"

"But I'm sort of terrified."

He wasn't sure what terrified her, but he had no doubts they could work through it. "Just being 'sort of terrified' sounds good to me. I mean, you like the idea of me being in love with you. *I* love the idea of being in love with you. This is a good place to be, right?"

"Ya, and it only took four years of marriage, three children, and one kind husband to get here."

Had he been kind? He wanted to be. He'd like to make up for her lousy childhood, but it was hard to give someone wings to fly when marriage and young children came with so many restraints.

Joel studied her, soaking in the moment. Her eyes were locked on his. She looked content, as if he'd removed heavy weights from her. What had he been thinking, standing out here in the dark talking to Gertie? Or changing Rose's home without asking her what she wanted and without explaining his intentions. He wouldn't make those mistakes again, and he had to stop Erma from causing more trouble. Life had plenty of that without help from an angry, bitter woman.

"Mama!" Mose called from inside.

"The children are up." Joel made the silly observation.

"Ya." She wasted no time going toward the house.

Joel took a few long strides to come up beside her and slid his hand into hers.

The house was a flurry of activity and noise as Rose and Joel cleaned up the breakfast dishes. She'd hardly touched her food, and she was pretty sure her feet weren't touching the ground. He loved her? Her heart was still pounding so hard she could feel it in her fingertips. This was everything she'd longed for. Wow. But the news was going to take some time to absorb, because right now her mind kept saying it couldn't be true. How could she have gotten everything so wrong?

She filled the mostly empty pot of grits with water. Joel put his hands on her shoulders and leaned in. He kissed her cheek before he wrapped his arms around her from behind and held her. "Care to look at the unfinished bedroom with me?"

The boys were in their room getting dressed for school, and Grace was in the living room playing with dolls.

Rose nodded, rinsed her hands, and grabbed a towel.

It seemed silly now that she'd been so upset about the room rather than talking to him. They communicated well about so many things, but honesty about how they felt and what they wanted was too awkward—much like the sex talk a Mamm was supposed to have with her daughter before she married. Sometimes it was just easier to pretend nothing needed to be said.

When she hated the idea of the room, it had seemed too far from the children. Now she liked the idea. She and Joel could have the space they needed to build this part of their married life.

Joel removed the towels at the foot of the doors that were keeping cold air out. He grabbed his coat off a chair and opened one of the double doors. Bitterly cold air whooshed through the room, flowing like a breezeway from one window opening to the next. There were exterior walls but no insulation or Sheetrock for interior walls and no glass in the windows. Joel put his coat around her shoulders, and they stepped into the room. He left the door open an inch, and she knew he'd done that so they could hear if the children called to them.

She looked around. "It's huge." He'd added two good-sized closets.

"Room for a large bed, a small couch, and built-in bookshelves."

She walked to a trapezoid-shaped metal insert. "A fireplace?"

"Eventually. You hate the cold and love fires." He crouched, touching a cable in the wall. "This is a gas starter, so you'll light it like the burners on the gas range. It'll have gas logs."

"Like in Elise's living room?" She sounded like a kid at Christmas. It was a pretty wonderful surprise.

"Ya, except I noticed that Elise's has an electric starter, and you'll have to strike a match or lighter to ignite it."

Her chest ached from excitement and guilt. He'd worked hard, trying to reach her heart and communicate his feelings, and she'd been nothing but difficult. "I . . . I don't have any words."

"Imagine that." He grinned.

She walked around the room, inspecting it. The views, the fireplace, the huge closets, and the extra space—it was perfect. "I feel horrible for being so ungrateful and blind to all you were doing."

"Ya, well, you dealt with me living in that state for the better part of two years. I've seen your many sides, and you've seen mine, and we're good for each other even when we're at our worst."

Her heart turned a flip. Seemed as if they'd both learned what real love was. She nodded at him as if what he'd said hadn't made the walls inside her quake. Would he dismantle them one day? Would she wake one morning to discover she no longer lived inside a prison?

Something caught her eye. "Pipes?"

"A bathroom. It'll be small, but—"

"You're going to spoil me."

"Ya, probably not." He rubbed the back of his neck. "You're not the kind to take anything for granted, and God help the human who aims to get you to work less. But I'd like to try to spoil you. That sounds like fun."

A carriage pulled into the driveway, and Rose realized it was getting late. School would begin soon, and Joel needed to get the boys there and go on to work. Marcus, Joel's Daed, was the driver, but who was the man beside him? She turned to Joel, knowing he'd answer her question without her needing to ask it.

Without missing a beat he looked out the glassless window. "A few days ago Daed said there was a new preacher in one of the Pennsylvania districts, and he was coming to Forest Hill to visit and preach. My guess is that's him. But I don't know why they're here. Maybe just for an introduction."

She went to the kitchen to prepare something to offer them.

Joel headed for the front door but paused at the foot of the steps and hollered, "Boys, it's time to get your coats, book bags, and lunches. You've got five minutes." He strode to the door, arriving there within moments of the knock. "Well, good morning, Daed. This is a surprise." He held the door open wide, welcoming both men.

"Joel, this is Thomas, the visiting preacher I told you about."

Joel shook the man's hand. "Kumm."

Rose set a basket of apples and oranges on the kitchen table. She would slice some cheese and offer coffee and coffeecake in a few minutes.

"This is my wife, Rose. Rose, this is Preacher Thomas."

She wiped her hands on a towel and nodded. "Welcome. Would you care for some coffee?"

Marcus shook his head. "We need to speak to Joel in private. Do you mind?"

The request wasn't unusual. The Dienner men were leaders in the community, and they often removed themselves from the family when they spoke about business.

Rose glanced at her husband, and he seemed as surprised as she was that there would be a meeting this morning. "Sure. I'll take the boys to school, and Grace can ride with us. Actually, I have a favor to ask of you too." She glanced at Joel, hoping he didn't mind.

Marcus dropped his hat. "A favor?" He grabbed it off the floor. "You've never asked for anything, Rose. Whatever you need, it's yours."

"*Gut,* denki. Would you, and any other men who have

time this week, give Joel a hand in finishing the addition? I'd really like for it to be done by Christmas."

He paused a moment before nodding. "Absolutely, Rose. It's yours. But that only gives us four days, so men will be traipsing through your front door and kitchen during a busy week of baking and Christmas preparations."

"It'll be worth it." Rose turned to Joel. "I'd like to go by Elise's to see if she has time for a visit. If she's not there or is too busy, I'll take Grace to the dry-goods store, giving you men a little uninterrupted time."

When Rose came out of the house, Joel ushered the children into the rig. His wife scurried toward it, and he put a blanket across the children's legs. "You boys learn a lot today, and be good for your teacher."

Grace grinned. "Mama says that one day I'll be big enough to go too."

He touched the tip of her nose. "Ya, too soon, I think."

Joel strode to the far side of the rig and opened the door for Rose. "Did you get some cash, just in case you need it?"

"Ya." Rose looked up at him. "Busy morning."

Joel chuckled. "Good morning, though, right?"

"The best." Rose clutched his hand and gave it a squeeze.

His heart pounded. "The best."

"You don't mind that I asked that favor of your Daed, do you?"

"I was proud of you for doing that, and to have it finished by Christmas"—he grinned, squeezing her hand—"priceless." Christmas was definitely their season.

"Take off work for the rest of the week, Joel. December and January are usually our slowest business months. We could use the time together to unwind, reset, and enjoy Christmas week while getting the room done."

"Ya, you're right. We need some time, and we've yet to finish making the children's barn and barnyard for Christmas."

"Deal?" She thrust her hand toward him.

"Deal." He shook it, closed the door, and waved as the buggy left the driveway. He returned to the house and removed his coat and hat. "Can I get you some more coffee?"

"We're fine." His Daed used his serious bishop tone.

Joel examined the preacher sitting at the table beside his Daed. He was dressed as if today were a Sunday meeting day. An uncomfortable silence filled the room, and his Daed motioned for Joel to take a seat across from him.

Joel sat. "So what's this visit about?"

"I had a conversation with Erma last night. She came to my place directly after leaving here." Daed almost whispered the words.

"Wonderful." Joel didn't roll his eyes, but he wanted to.

"She's brought something to my, well, to our attention."

Joel stiffened, and he found it hard to breathe. Whatever Erma had said, he hoped she wasn't spreading it throughout the community. "Our?"

"Preacher Thomas and me. It's just between Erma and us for now."

Joel stared into the preacher's eyes, wondering why he had been pulled into this, whatever *this* was. "Are you going to tell me what Erma brought to your attention?"

The preacher shifted in his chair. "She believes you haven't consummated your marriage."

"Excuse me?" Joel clenched his fingers. What had he done? In his desire to defend his wife to Erma, he'd shared their most private secret.

"Don't get upset with him, Son. Erma came to the house and spoke with me alone. But it's a heavy topic, and I thought it best that I talk to him."

"And Erma's gossip grants you the right to share the gossip with a stranger?"

His Daed looked regretful, but he sat up straight. "There's no need to be hostile."

"I'm not hostile. I'm annoyed. There is a difference."

Daed rubbed his forehead. "I'm sorry if you feel we've been inappropriate in our conversations about your private life, but quite honestly, Joel, what Erma said came as a shock. The relationship between man and wife is one that the community cares about deeply. It is part of how we obey God's commands and sustain our faith. I never imagined that after four years your marriage to Rose wasn't, uh, intimate."

Joel looked down at the table. Was this conversation really happening? After the magical moments with Rose earlier?

"When did you marry Rose?" the visiting preacher asked.

"A week after my wife died."

"And why did you do that?"

He shook his head, wondering if it was a trick question. "I had two little ones and a newborn. Have you ever seen a newborn survive without constant, round-the-clock care? I haven't." He tried to keep his tone matter-of-fact.

"Was that the only reason?"

The man's questioning made Joel remember an Englisch friend talking about police interrogations. Apparently whatever a person said could and would be used against him in a court of law. He had never been to court, but he imagined this is what it felt like. "You two want to get to the point? I fail to see how what Rose and I do behind closed doors is of interest to anyone but us—and apparently Erma."

Daed sighed. "Son, I don't want to bring grief or hurt. I blame myself because I rushed you into this marriage. In hindsight I realize I didn't consider much of anything other than getting the pressure off your Mamm and Erma. Now . . . if you and Rose haven't slept together—"

"How is that anyone's business?" Joel couldn't believe he'd been so careless as to disclose this information to Erma. Rose would die of shame.

His Daed's face turned slightly red. "Is that yes or no?"

Joel didn't say anything and looked back down to the table again.

The preacher shifted. "I've never heard of any Amish who have been in such a situation before. But under such circumstances we believe an annulment may be permitted."

"What?" Joel pushed away from the table, stood up, and backed away from the men.

"When both married parties—"

Joel put his hands up, cutting the preacher off. "I know what the word means. I just couldn't believe I'd heard correctly."

"I can't make any promises, but you and Rose might be able to dissolve the union without causing much scandal," Daed said softly.

"Dissolve it? *You* told me to marry her. I want to be married to her!"

"I know, but now I think I made the wrong decision. We know Rose better and the home life that drove her to us. If the church feels that an annulment is the right thing, that the union is not honoring to God, then she could start over, and you could find a more suitable woman."

Joel's emotions were in a stewpot, spattering and boiling over. He began to pace. "I can find one more suitable?" *This is what Rose often feels like. The world is suddenly insensible, and all words are trapped inside.*

Daed looked away. "We're not saying Rose isn't a fine girl. I love her, but what if my decision about your marriage set her life on a course that could be very wrong? You two haven't made a physical commitment to each other, and there has to be a reason for that."

Joel found his tongue. "We're a family. What are you thinking? Do you have any idea what it would do to your grandchildren to lose the only mother they apparently remember? Besides, she's made more of a commitment than you know. And she loves Mose, Levi, and Grace as if they were her own."

Daed nodded. "I know, and I hate the thought of the pain that her leaving would cause. But not consummating your vows for four years? That doesn't strike me as just an unhappy marriage but also one that's not interested in multiplying. As I'm the one who insisted on it, I must try to make this right for everyone. Since she's a mother to the children, maybe she would choose to stay in Forest Hill. But would you make that decision for her because of your children?"

Joel's heart seemed to stop, and his mind played a series of unrelated images. He wanted to tell them that Rose would never choose to leave, that she loved him, but his lips were as numb as his body. If given the right to leave, she would choose to stay with him, wouldn't she? Crossing back to the table, he took a seat again.

"Son, talk to her about this. Explain the situation, and let her choose. Your Mamm and I will pray without ceasing that she chooses to be your wife as God meant the relationship to be."

The preacher drummed the table with his thumb. "The decision will not be left in your Daed's hands. Clearly he's too invested to look at this objectively. As men of God, the bishop and preachers in my community will take time to figure out whether we can, in good conscience, allow a marriage to be annulled. Vows were made—but to become one and produce children for the good of the community and the faith. You and Rose have not fulfilled that obligation, whatever your reasons."

Joel looked out of the corner of his eye at the preacher, and the man went quiet.

Daed cleared his throat. "Now that I've said my piece about the annulment and Rose, let me add that I'm bringing this to you first. The issue must be discussed, but we thought you should know and that Rose should—"

Joel couldn't control his anger. "No!"

Silence fell. Neither the preacher nor his Daed pressed to speak. Joel's rib cage seemed to lift from his body, and a pulsing sensation swayed in his chest as if his heart were a pendulum attached to a string. He couldn't look at them, and he certainly couldn't allow them to talk to Rose about an annulment. He might not be able to stop their investigating whether the details of his and Rose's marriage were in line with the *Ordnung,* but the mere suggestion of their marriage being dissolved could put Rose into an emotional nosedive. Considering how upset she had been by the arrival of a pretty widow and his building an addition to the house, he didn't know how she'd handle it.

Joel looked past the two men and stared at the wall. Every ounce of him wanted to say, "She's happy, it's a good marriage, and we'll consummate the marriage soon." But for some reason he couldn't force the declaration from his lips. Was his Daed right that he should talk to Rose about it and let her decide? She loved him—he believed that. But given the choice to undo her life with him, a choice no other Amish was ever allowed, would she take it?

Joel cleared his voice. "How long before a decision is made?"

"A few weeks, maybe a month."

That would at least get them through Christmas. Then he could find the right moment to talk to her about the annulment conversation. He had to pick the right time.

Joel tried to swallow, but his mouth was too dry. He didn't want to lose Rose and didn't think the church should be forcing such a terrible ultimatum on them. *She loves me, doesn't she,*

God? "I don't want anyone to breathe a word about this to Rose. I have to be the one to talk to her about it."

Daed stood. "I'm sorry, Joel. This is my fault. I pushed you and Rose into this. The Amish don't get everything right, but we have traditions in place to make sure singles get to choose their spouse."

Joel remained at the table. He thought about the morning's excitement over the bedroom and the idea of consummating their wedding vows in the near future. Now he had to offer her a "get out of jail free" card? He could envision her retreating within herself, hearing belittling words that were never said or intended.

Joel heard muffled movements, and someone mumbled, "We know the way out."

The thought of not being with Rose was entirely too frightening. The string snapped, but his heart began to beat again. His body and lips were no longer numb.

He could feel everything.

The horse slowed as Rose pulled the rig up to Elise's house. Snow continued to fall, and the gray and white of winter yielded to the pretty Christmas lights and decorations that seemed to fill Elise's property. Her friend's house looked like a picture from an Englischer Christmas magazine. Strings of multicolored lights wound around the gutters and chimney, and several inflatable characters—snowmen, reindeer, and Santa Claus—waved side to side with the wind. Flashing lights in the shape of icicles hung off the porch. The large cherry tree in the front yard, which in a few months would have its own natural adornment of blooms, had hundreds of lights wrapped around its trunk and branches. Grace sat on the anchored booster seat, covered in a wool blanket, looking out the frosty window.

"Oooh!" Grace clapped her hands. "Look, she has new blow-up snowmen."

"Ya, she does."

Every year Elise and her family expanded their outdoor Christmas decorations. Elise once said her husband made it his yearly quest to delight their children with new outdoor Christmas surprises, even though it took several days to set them up and take them down.

Elise was Joel's age and the only veterinarian for miles, but she had scaled back her work after her first child was born. When needed, she filled in for the vet in Hinton, and she tended to the Amish community's livestock.

From the first time Rose met her, she knew they had the potential to become good friends. But she'd never expected them to get as comfortable with each other as they had. Rose pulled the rig under the shelter and helped Grace out. She then tossed a blanket over the horse, removed the bridle, and replaced it with a harness.

"Look, Mama!" Grace had hurried to the inflatables and was squishing a scarf-wearing penguin and laughing.

"Careful," Rose warned. Just how much punishment could the penguin take?

"Don't worry," Elise's voice carried from somewhere. "Skipper has proved himself quite hearty. My girls haven't destroyed that penguin in three years." Elise stood in the doorway of her home, waving at Grace and Rose while pulling on boots. Most people would wait inside where it was warm, but not Elise. "Did I know you were coming this morning and forgot?"

"No. Is it okay?"

"Love it." Her friend continued walking toward her until they met on the lawn. She ran a hand through her straight blond hair, pulling it out of her coat, and then covered her head with the hood. "Saves me time. My mom picked up the girls a few minutes ago so I could go shopping without them. I was planning to come by your place in a bit, hoping to convince you and Miss Grace to go shopping with me."

Rose had forgotten the Englisch got at least two weeks off from school over the holidays. Since Christmas Eve and Day took place on the weekend this year, her boys would be off only the day after Christmas for the tradition of Second Christmas. That was it.

"Ya, we'll go." Why not get some shopping done while they visited? "I just need to borrow your cell so I can leave a message for Joel, and we'll have to be back to pick the boys up from school." Although shopping together would be fun, maybe she should ask if they could just stay at Elise's house, given the sensitive and rather embarrassing subjects she wanted to talk about.

Elise passed her cell to Rose before holding out her hand to Grace. "Any little girls out here who'd like to see a litter of pups?"

"Me!" Grace ran to Elise and grabbed her hand. The three of them went toward the barn.

"Another rescue mission?" Rose scrolled through Elise's short list of favorites until she came to her own name.

"Yeah, the MacDonalds brought them to me yesterday. They were headed back from Lewisburg and found them in a box alongside the road. With it being Christmas, surely we can find homes for all of them."

Rose nodded, pressed the Call button, and left a message on the machine. She and Elise fed the livestock while Grace played with the pups, and then after the hour drive they pulled into the mall parking lot. Rose repeatedly tried to approach Elise with the things on her mind, but her mouth had yet to cooperate with her will. How did Joel put up with such nonsense? Her chest tightened, and a smile threatened to break free. He didn't just put up with it. He loved her.

They rented a fire-engine stroller to contain Grace, and with only two snack breaks, they had everything Elise needed within ninety minutes.

Elise held up the bags. "See, you are good at this."

"Give me other people's money, and I have no trouble spending it." Rose had bought a few things too, items Joel would want her to get for the children for Christmas.

"So let's talk. What's going on?"

Rose pointed at Grace. "This little one is a mimic. We need to distract her."

"There's a cute indoor playground on the level below us. We could stop and get some hot tea at the shop next to it and talk while Grace plays."

Rose nibbled her lip. "I can't go home without answers. I just can't."

"Come on, then. Let's go talk." Elise pushed Grace's fire engine, laden with the small child and all the shopping bags, toward the tea shop.

Several minutes later Rose and Elise sat at a small table, one of twenty tables that were positioned strategically around the children's play area. The playground was geared to give little ones five and under a place to burn off energy during a shopping trip with their parents. Soft-foam climbing structures were shaped like a caterpillar, mushrooms, and a race car, and a slide was designed to look like a waterfall. Grace had already made a friend and was running and playing chase with her.

Rose tasted her "fancy tea," as Elise called it. "Well. You were right about how Joel sees Gertie. I was worrying over nothing."

"Of course I was right." Elise flashed her a smile and a wink. "I know Joel well enough, and he's one of the good guys. Added to that, he loves you."

"I . . . think he does. I mean, you've been saying that, but today he said it."

"Yes!" Elise raised her fist into the air. "Yes! I knew it. Come on. Tell me more."

"He . . . he . . . seems to find me attractive."

Elise leaned in closer and gestured up and down at Rose. "And why wouldn't he? Look at you!"

Rose's cheeks burned. She raised her hands to cover them until the flush left her face. "I don't know about that." She shrugged. "I don't think I've ever felt attractive in my life, except . . ."

One of Elise's eyebrows raised in interest. "Except . . ."

"Well, sometimes when Joel and I are alone in the living room, sitting on the couch with candle lights flickering or a fire in the hearth, we talk for hours, and then after all has been said, he wraps his arm so gently around my shoulders . . ." Rose couldn't figure a way to describe these particular feelings.

Elise arched her brows. "I knew I liked that man. He's got moves. So tell me, what's the holdup on sleeping with him?"

Rose closed her eyes, trying to gain some composure. Leave it to Elise to jump straight to the matter without any embarrassment.

"It's complicated." Rose took a breath to steady her emotions. "Lots of mixed emotions swirling inside me."

"Pick the one that scares you the most."

"I don't know, honestly. I guess I'm afraid he'll be disappointed." She lowered her eyes to her teacup. "He and Florence had such a connection. What if he compares me to her and I don't measure up? What if he regrets taking our relationship to that physical level but feels pressured to keep going ahead with it? What if he never feels anything with me that compares to what he felt with Florence? They had years together, and I'm a second-class wife he's learned to love." She raised her eyes.

Elise stared at her. She blinked several times. "First, 'pressured to keep going ahead' with making love? Usually not a man's problem. And second, is your lack of self-confidence a bottomless pit?"

Rose sighed. "Ya, pretty much."

Elise leaned forward and put her hands around Rose's. "He wants to build a life with *you.* He's being honest with how he feels about *you.* That's enough, for Pete's sake. Stop second-guessing what he wants or what he's thinking. Stop being terrified." Elise grinned, giving her a wicked look. "Actually, it's time to open up, girl. Seduce the poor man, which should take you all of five minutes after the kids are asleep. Hey, you remember our conversation about the birds and the bees and what to do to avoid pregnancy?"

Rose's cheeks flushed again. This is why she wanted to talk

to Elise, to hear her friend's candid thoughts about such topics, but in this moment she wished they were in a more private setting.

"Ya. Shh." Rose covered her lips with her index finger.

"I'm not being loud, and no one's paying any attention to our conversation. It's shop 'til you drop here. You're just being self-conscious. What I'm saying is that if you surprise him with an ounce of boldness, he won't be thinking of anyone but you. And he won't forget that night, ever."

Was that true? Could it be possible for her, a woman of twenty-five with zero experience in *that* department, to give the man she loves a true night to remember?

"Oh." Elise's eyes lit up. "Let's give Grace another few minutes to play while we finish our tea. Then I have an idea of just where to begin to help you feel more confident."

"Hmm?" Rose pulled from her thoughts.

Elise gestured at a store across from them. The boutique sign said Lavender's, and the mannequins in the window were dressed in undergarments and nightgowns. Rose shook her head.

"I don't think I can do that."

Joel hadn't moved since his Daed and Preacher Thomas left. His eyes were fixed on the same space on the wall. If he knew what to pray for, he would. The right moment to talk to Rose? For her to hear what he was saying, that never in a million years would he want her to go? That the bishops and preachers had no say in their love for each other?

Could they make Rose move out? She loved Mose, Levi, and Grace as if they were hers, so the worst-case scenario would be that his wife changed her mind about being intimate with him, and the marriage would be annulled because they were living outside the church's mandate for wedded couples. Maybe the mandates from the church were a real issue, but Joel wondered if the problem stemmed from Daed being the bishop. His

Daed feared that he'd used his position of influence and power to force a desperate young woman to take a forever vow. But even if the worst happened and they annulled the marriage, Joel believed Rose would live nearby so the children could be a part of her days. Maybe he'd have to court her as a young single man would. It seemed absurd, but he wasn't above jumping through hoops if it meant having a "real" marriage with Rose.

His legs tingled, objecting to his staying in one place for so long. What time was it?

He looked at the mantel clock, but something seemed off. No doubt he'd been sitting here for hours, but the clock was stuck on 8:30, about the time Rose left with the children.

A spark ignited inside him, like a lighter finally creating a flame, a source of enough heat to get him out of his chair. He walked to the clock, picked it up, and went straight out the front door and to his workshop. He opened the round, brass backing. An array of fitted parts stared back at him—a back plate, a series of cogs, the pendulum, the gear train, and main springs, among other pieces. As with a good marriage, each piece had to fit in order for things to run smoothly. Each cog worked in succession with the one next to it, and that kept the pendulum moving properly so the clock kept time.

It had quit four years ago within hours of Florence's passing, and he had fixed it later that week. In the years since it had worked perfectly, never giving him any more trouble—until now. The muscles in his shoulders tightened, and the tension moved up the back of his neck. He had to get it working again.

He pulled out the inner workings and tested each cog to see what the problem was. When the mainspring seemed fine, he returned his attention to the cogs. He heard a carriage pull onto the driveway, and when he glanced up, his children were running toward the house. School was out already? How long had he been tinkering with the clock? He returned his focus to it.

"Joel?" Rose called as she walked into the shop. "Hey."

"The mantel clock stopped again. Did you know it wasn't working?"

She moved closer. "It was working fine yesterday." She held up small brown shopping bags. "I bought Christmas decorations for the house. I know we can't put up too much. But I bought some scented candles, greenery to go around them, and a string of lights that I thought would go well in the new room. The lights are battery powered, and I know we aren't supposed to have them up, but we can keep it between ourselves, right?"

He recognized how excited she sounded, more excited than she'd been in a long while, but all he could think about was fixing the clock. He fixated on one tiny cog that wasn't connecting to any other cogs. What would've caused that to shift?

"Joel?"

It was then he realized what she had asked. "Ya, I think the lights will be fine." Whatever Rose wanted, he would give it to her. What he most wanted to give her was complete ignorance about the annulment discussion. Would that be dishonest of him? He'd found the issue with the cog that wasn't turning. The pivot was loose, and the cog had shifted.

"Something wrong?"

The excitement in her voice had died down, and he looked up. "Sorry. The clock isn't working again."

The timing had him spooked. It had quit when he lost Florence. But it wasn't rational to feel this uptight over a timepiece.

Rose set the bags on the floor. "What did your Daed and that preacher want?"

He should've already thought about what he would tell her. "Nothing."

"Nothing?"

The words weren't coming to him. He put the pointed slant tweezers in the gap between two cogs. "Just needed to talk about some things Erma brought up to Daed."

Silence. Joel tried to ease the cog into place, praying he was doing this right. What did he know about clock repair?

"That explains you being out here alone, mumbling to yourself. Did you make plans with them about working on the bedroom?"

"Not yet." How was he going to keep such a secret from her? He had just opened up and told her how he felt, and now he had to hide the truth again? "It may need to wait. We have to consider the men's schedules with it being Christmas in five days. And you and I haven't even finished the big present for the children."

It was mostly done, but he would need at least four more hours to complete it. He and Rose had made a two-story wooden barn, eighteen inches tall and two feet long, with a split-rail fence to create a barnyard. The doors and gates all opened, and he'd bought a set of beautifully carved horses, cows, and chickens from an Amish friend. The children would spend endless hours playing with it in the living room, especially in the long winter months. He treasured that kind of time with his family and Rose by his side. But what kind of tension would fill the coming evenings as he held back his father's announcement?

The crinkling of paper drew him from his thoughts. Rose held out a box to him. "I got something for you. An early Christmas present."

Joel took a breath and looked up from the clock. "Did you?"

She opened it and looped her slender fingers through a pair of silky black straps and then lifted a short, lacy gown from the box.

His heart cinched. She was being vulnerable and sweet. "I . . . uh . . . don't know how to break this to you, but I don't think it will fit me."

Rose laughed. She lifted his chin, leaned down, and pressed

her lips against his. Joel stood and wrapped his arms around her, kissing her, wishing this moment was free of secrets.

She lowered her head. "Wow."

"Ya. Wow." He should've told her sooner how he felt. Maybe then they wouldn't be in this fix.

She rested her head on his chest.

"I love you, Rose."

She shifted, putting her lips near his ear. "After the children are asleep, I could show you how well this fits me."

Joel took a deep breath. What could he say? "Well . . ."

Rose pulled back, looking in his eyes, and he saw her confusion and unmistakable hurt. "You're hesitant?"

"About us, no. I promise. I just feel I should finish the room. Our bedroom." He tried to pull her back into the embrace.

"Okay." Rose dropped the nightgown into the bag, leaving the box on the workbench. She gathered the other shopping bags and left without another word. Joel sat there alone with a broken clock and a box marked "Lavender's."

He focused on the workings of the clock again, picking up the tweezers and putting them right where the problem cog was. He applied gentle pressure, but the cog didn't move. Frustrated, he put some muscle into making the cog connect properly.

The cog snapped and flew out, leaving a gap where Joel had been working.

Mixing chocolate, cream cheese, and other ingredients in a bowl, Rose breathed deep. Her home smelled of Christmastime, and with good reason. In three days it would be Christmas Eve. Grace was on a chair beside Rose, her four-year-old hands holding a small hammer as she smashed Oreo cookies in a plastic baggie.

Mose and Levi were in the new addition, *helping* Joel and their granddad, along with four other men. The boys had gone to school today, and they would go again tomorrow and Friday, but they were enjoying helping the men work when home.

A fire roared in the hearth. The earth was covered in a white blanket, with more snow expected tomorrow. The stack of glistening presents on the window seat in the living room kept growing little by little.

This year was working toward being the best Christmas she'd ever had, despite whatever was nagging Joel.

Grace whacked the hammer against the Oreos again and giggled. "I just mash 'em up good." She tapped the hammer against the broken cookie pieces.

"Ya, you do." Rose put her arm around Grace. "You're such a good helper."

Grace never looked up. "I know. What will you do without me once I'm in school?"

"I don't know, but your confidence is a gift to me all on its own."

"What's confidence?"

"That warm feeling in your belly that says you're good at things."

Before coming to Forest Hill, Rose had a few fleeting moments of confidence. It was a wonderful feeling, even though for her it was a hard-fought-for sentiment. She wanted the children to believe in themselves.

Grace looked up. "I'm good at lots of stuff."

"Very true." And she was. Rose wouldn't support false confidence, but all three children were bright and skilled in many things for their age.

She *would* miss little Grace's constant help the day she joined her big brothers in school. But that day was not today.

For now her little daughter, at age four, was perfectly content to mix ingredients with Mama in the kitchen.

"What's next, Mama?" Grace put her finger on the recipe for Double Chocolate Cheesecake in the open cookbook. The book gave a simplified version of the recipe, which made it perfect for Grace to help Rose.

"Hmm, let's see." Rose picked up the *Feed My Sheep* cookbook from the counter. "We need to put the crushed cookies in a bowl and add melted butter." Rose slid a bowl in front of Grace.

"I can do it, Mama."

"Okay."

Grace opened the baggie and slowly poured the cookie pieces into the bowl.

Years ago Elise's mom had put together this family cookbook, and Elise gave it to Rose the first month she was here. It had several short-cut oriented, tasty recipes that fed a lot of people. That alone was very helpful since she was providing lunch and snacks for all the men who were helping Joel finish the bedroom.

"Let's add the melted butter." Rose poured the golden liquid over the Oreos.

"I want to stir all by myself!" Grace grabbed the wooden spoon and seemed to use all her strength to move the utensil through the mixture. The Oreo crumbs slowly took on an even darker color as the butter saturated them.

Rose had been waiting a long time to make a certain recipe in this book—Italian Cream Cake. If all went as planned, it would be part of Joel's Christmas present, a type of wedding cake. There would be cause for privately eating wedding cake at some point over the next few days, wouldn't there?

She thought so, but something had bothered him since he spoke with his Daed and that preacher. He would talk to her about it when he was ready. Was the old heartache once again waking? Losing a loved one as he had came with a world of grief, and that didn't disappear simply because he'd fallen in love again. She understood that. She had already accepted that on occasions, even years from now, he would still have seasons of coping with the loss. Especially as the children grew and parts of Florence would be mirrored in their traits.

Nevertheless, she was giddy with excitement. Twenty-five years old and absolutely giddy. It was a first, although each Christmas since she'd arrived here had been better than the previous one, and all of them were much better than the mess she'd grown up in. Still, she'd written her Mamm a warm letter, telling about her life and choosing which of the good memories to share with her.

"Now let's press the mixture into this pan." Rose helped Grace pour the buttered crumbs into a cake pan lined with foil.

They both pressed their fingers into the mixture that looked like garden dirt, making it mold to the pan. "Now we put it in the oven to bake for ten minutes. This part you have to let me do." Rose kissed Grace's nose and set the kitchen timer.

Grace continued to play with the measuring cups and spoons as they waited for the timer to ding. After the crust was toasted and smelling great, the timer went off, and Rose removed the pan from the oven. Using rubber spatulas, she and Grace carefully scraped the filling from the mixing bowl into the crust. She placed the cake back in the oven and set the timer for forty-five minutes.

"When will I be big enough to open the oven? When I'm seven, like Mose?"

"Ya, maybe. We'll see. But I do need your help on something else: wrapping the last few gifts for your Daed."

The little girl's face lit up. Christmas for a child was pure magic. Even the mundane tasks like wrapping packages were fascinating. Rose lifted Grace off the chair she was standing on and twirled her around before setting her on her feet.

"Again, please!" her youngest squealed.

Rose smiled and obliged. "Boys,"—she set Grace's feet back on the ground—"let's get some packages wrapped."

"Ya!" Mose yelled as he and Levi ran out of the new addition and scurried up the stairs. "We gotta get the presents. Meet you in your room, Mama."

"Okay, I'll be there shortly, but slow down, please."

Joel came out of the unfinished bedroom, a hammer in hand and a lopsided smile lifting one side of his handsome face, his focus on her. "*You* wield some power."

His smile was genuine, but he still didn't seem fully at ease. She examined his face, trying not to think about how she craved another kiss.

She understood what he meant. He'd tried a few times to get the boys interested in doing something, anything outside of the work area. "Do I?" She pulled tape and scissors from the kitchen drawer. "You carry this." She passed the tape to Grace.

Grace scurried up the stairs.

Rose and Joel walked toward each other until they were inches apart. "If I don't hear the timer go off, would you holler up the stairs or get the cheesecake out of the oven for me?"

"I'm pretty sure I can manage that."

"Me too." She smiled up at him. "No eating any of it. Got it?"

"Hey, it's my house too," he teased, saying the same thing she'd said this morning about wanting to see the bedroom. He'd told her she couldn't peek until late tomorrow.

"Ya, ya, ya. Whatever." She mimicked a surly teen and went up the stairs.

Once she and the children were in her bedroom, Mose

slammed the door. "I thought you were never going to get done in the kitchen." Mose tossed his presents on the bed.

Rose pulled rolls of wrapping paper from the top of her closet, and the craziness began. By the time they were nearing the end, her back ached and her ears were ringing. What was it about Christmastime that caused children to forget how to use their inside voices?

"Mose!" Levi yelled across the wrapping-paper chaos. "I need the tape again!"

Wrapping presents with three young children took approximately ten times as long as it would have taken Rose by herself, but it was worth it to see the finished products the children came up with.

"Hold on. I'm still using it." Mose had added so much tape to the package that Rose was convinced Joel would need a pair of scissors to get into his gift. "Here." Mose threw the tape. Hard. It overshot his target, and at that same moment Joel opened the bedroom door. The tape smacked him in the chest. Rose burst into laughter as the children gasped.

"Whoa." He chuckled. "Guess I should have worn a hard hat before sticking my head in this construction zone." Joel picked up the tape from the floor and tossed it onto the bed.

"Daed! No peeking!" Grace stood on the bed, trying to shoo her father out of the room.

"Hey, I knocked first. No one heard me."

"Imagine that." Rose angled her head, lifted her brows, and nibbled on her bottom lip, flirting with him. "Grace, honey, I think all the gifts are covered very well at this point." The children had used about three times the amount of wrapping paper it should have taken, but she wasn't going to correct them when it had been so much fun.

"So what's up?" Rose asked.

Joel had slowly grown comfortable with this room. It'd been a process, one he said began when Rose started leaving the bedroom door open at night so all of them could talk to each other from their beds, or, in Joel's case, from the sectional couch in the former office down the hall. They would share an event and bid one another good night. After the children were asleep, Joel and she would talk just loudly enough to each other to be heard, share something normal, and then start laughing like teenagers at a sleepover. Elise called it "all very John-Boy and Walton's Mountain type of stuff," whatever that meant.

Joel shifted. "I removed the dessert from the oven about twenty minutes ago."

Had more than an hour passed already? "Denki."

"But I came upstairs to tell you that I think you all should go to the front porch."

He looked so attractive in that moment, teasing and prodding the children. She thought of what it would be like to embrace him whenever she wanted. When his eyes met hers, she saw longing mixed with something indefinable. She didn't know why he couldn't simply tell her what had been on his mind since the ministers came to see him on Tuesday, but she knew he was in love with her. That helped a lot.

"To the porch?" Mose scowled. "It's cold out there."

"Grab your coat and put on your boots. I think you'll find the treat worth it," Joel said.

Grace's eyes grew large. "A treat!"

All three children clamored for the bedroom door, and Rose tagged behind. The children were soon stomping down the stairs, but Rose seemed glued in place as she studied her husband.

He gestured down the hallway. "After you."

As she started to pass him, he caught her arm. "Gertie's here. I just wanted to warn you."

"Hmm." Rose punched his shoulder with her finger. "I need a kiss. A good one to cope with this properly."

Amusement and pleasure gleamed in his eyes. He mocked a sigh. "I suppose."

But when he wrapped his arms around her and put his mouth on hers, there was no hint of humoring her. The kiss lingered, and when she rested her hands on his chest, she could feel his heart racing.

"Mama! Daed!" Levi's voice rumbled from the foot of the stairs. "We got our coats on. Can we go out now?"

"Wait for us," Rose answered, but she didn't pull away from him.

He smiled, took her by the hand, and led her down the stairs. "There are people waiting. Kumm." Joel grabbed his coat, and Rose did the same. With his children standing ready at the door, Joel opened it. There was a gathering of children and adults positioned in a small arc on their lawn. Gertie was among them and looked to be the leader, as all eyes were on her. She took a breath, and they began singing, "Away in a manger, no crib for a bed, the little Lord Jesus laid down his sweet head."

"That's my favorite!" Grace whispered excitedly as she tugged on Rose's arm. All of them moved onto the porch, and Rose pulled Grace closer as her family stood listening to the singing. Joel put his arm around Rose's shoulders. She let the peace of the songs seep into her soul.

When the carolers finished and silence hung in the air, Rose released Grace from her embrace and clapped, and the rest of her family joined her. After they applauded, Rose motioned to the visitors, whose cheeks and noses were turning red from the cold. "Kumm on in."

"Ya, please do. Rose and Grace have filled the house with cookies and desserts." Joel opened the front door and ushered

Rose inside first and then the rest. "And the men and I could use a break from working on the addition."

"I'll have coffee for the adults and hot chocolate for the children in just a few minutes." Rose's words were for no one in particular as she hurried to put another pot of coffee on to brew.

The room rumbled with laughter and silly stories as Rose and Joel served everyone a hot beverage and cookies. When almost everyone had their beverage and chosen dessert on a plate, Joel turned to hand out another mug of coffee. "Do you see anyone else who needs a drink?" He scouted the room.

"Gertie." Rose nodded to a corner where Gertie sat by herself, watching others interact.

"Uh . . . not me," Joel whispered. "It's too cold outside for a mud bath."

"Give me that." She winked at Joel and walked toward Gertie.

Now that everything was out in the open, Gertie no longer seemed like a threat but rather a woman who was currently experiencing crushing loneliness—something Rose was familiar with. Maybe they could become friends.

She crossed the room and handed the cup to Gertie. "The singing was lovely."

"Denki." Gertie stared into her mug.

"'Away in a Manger' is Grace's favorite carol. She thinks it's funny that Jesus was once a little baby sleeping where animals feed."

Gertie perked up a bit. "Ya, it's my youngest daughter's favorite too."

Their conversation continued, both sharing little idiosyncrasies about their children. It was funny to Rose how parents never ran out of cute stories about their children.

When their conversation waned, Gertie looked thoughtful. "About the other day and the conversations I had with your husband before that"—she drew a shaky breath—"I didn't mean anything . . . inappropriate." She sighed and looked at the mug in her hands. "I just . . . It seems no one really understands the grief I'm dealing with. It feels suffocating at times. Joel and I never talked about anything very important or deep, but it brought me some comfort to talk with him. I wasn't looking at him as a man but as a survivor of something I'm trying to survive."

Rose believed her. She now understood that the widow wouldn't have crossed those lines with a married man if she hadn't been through such a loss. Gertie's eyes finally met hers.

Rose placed her hand on the woman's shoulder. "I do understand. Really. Though I never knew Florence, I saw the depth of sadness that her absence created in Joel, the children, and the whole community. You're not as alone as it feels."

Gertie's eyes misted. "Denki."

"I think we should get to know each other a little better."

Gertie blinked. "I'd like that." She seemed a little bolstered. "Would you and yours like to join the other carolers? We have room in the wagon sleigh, and we're visiting at least two more homes tonight."

Rose had a dozen things she needed to do, including wrapping presents for the children and cleaning up the kitchen from the carolers' snacking. Christmas Eve was in a few days, and after spending all day with Elise yesterday, she was dreadfully behind.

But nothing was as important as making memories with Joel and the children. What better way to do it than riding in a sleigh with friends and family and singing carols about Christ's birth?

"I love the idea." She scanned the room, looking for Joel. When she spotted him, he was watching her, and their eyes locked. She pointed to the carolers, then to him and herself, and then used her fingers to make a walking motion and pointed out the door.

He laughed and made monkey motions with his hands, as if he'd understood nothing she'd tried to convey. He walked over to her.

"I was asking if we could join the carolers."

"I know. I was just messing with you." He put his hand around hers. "Ya, sure we can go. You name it, and it's yours until Christmas is over."

"I get a repeat next Christmas, right?"

A flicker of anxiety reflected in his eyes, but he smiled. "If you say so, Rose."

Waning sunlight spilled across the snowy hill. Joel paused, soaking in the moment. The hillside and surrounding pastureland had footprints and sled tracks that he and his family had made over the last three hours. His children's laughter echoed inside him as they waved and began the walk to the house.

"Ya," Rose whispered, half out of breath as she dragged an empty sled to the top of the hill. "It's pretty great."

He hadn't said anything, but she'd pegged his sentiments exactly.

She put the sled beside him. "My turn."

He laughed. The children had said those same words over and over again, asking him to ride with one of them. "Kumm." He straddled the sled and sat, just as he'd done dozens of times today. In a couple of days it would be Christmas Eve, and it would be a perfect one if he could free his mind of the burdensome secret.

Rose sat in front of him and snuggled against him. She leaned her head against his chest. "Listen, buddy. Go fast, and don't tip us over." Her breaths were frosty, and her cheeks matched her name.

"I was thinking more in line of shoving you off midway down as I zoom onward."

"Do it. I dare you."

"Nee, you would scream like a four-year-old, and the children would be mad at me," Joel teased as he put his legs around hers.

Rose tilted her head, pulled the knit scarf from her neck, and tapped her skin. Her boldness to let him know what she wanted made his heart thud. He leaned in and kissed her neck, nuzzling against the warmth and breathing in his wife. Did she have any idea how much he treasured who they were as a couple? Their friendship was even stronger than the unity of their parenting and family partnership. But he longed for more, for the next step with his wife of four years.

"Denki." She nodded her approval and replaced her scarf. "Now, let's go."

He lunged forward, giving the sled its needed start. They swooshed down the hill with Rose leaning against him, laughing as they went faster. And then the sled hit something under the snow and flew into the air. Joel held her tight, using all his strength to cling to her and to keep them on the sled. They landed with a thud and fell off the sled. The shock of the hard earth rattled Joel, and he said a quick prayer for Rose.

Sprawled on the ground facing skyward, Joel blinked and jerked air into his lungs. "You okay?"

"Afraid to get close enough to see for yourself?"

He smiled at her spunk, rolled over, and belly-crawled, closing the few inches between them. He propped himself up on his elbows and grinned as he leaned over her.

"Do over." She grabbed him by the coat collar. "That was not what I requested."

"Ride's over, lady." He kissed her cheek. "Deal with it."

She pulled him closer. "I will for a lip kiss."

"Hmm." Joel mocked as if he was considering it. She tugged on his coat until his lips were on hers, and he felt as if he were in a winter wonderland, a Christmastime dream he didn't want to wake from. He wanted her. To love and to cherish. To be lovers and best friends until the very end.

"That's it for you." She shoved him away. "We have children nearby. What are you thinking?" she teased.

He helped her up, and they crossed the field, watching the three little ones talk and laugh as they made their way toward home.

"Joel."

"Hmm?"

"I talked to Elise a while back, and I . . . I know how to avoid coming up pregnant in a natural way that the church won't object to. For the sake of family planning, I mean."

He stopped cold.

She shrugged. "If that's what's bothering you, and clearly something is. And when we do conceive, Elise said she or her husband would be willing to be on call to take us to the hospital as soon as I go into labor."

He couldn't find any words. When they began their new husband-and-wife life, it would be best to add to their family as soon as possible. That would be the quickest way to stop the church's interest in their marriage. But far more important than that, he wanted a child with Rose and to share that kind of happiness with her. The joy of having a baby, *their* baby, would mean far more to her than she probably knew right now.

She inched forward, looking up at him. "I just thought you might be worried about that."

He had considered it. It was natural to worry about childbirth and home births after what had happened to Florence.

"Can you say something?" she asked.

"Nope, I've been rendered speechless."

"Is the idea of having a baby what's bothering you?"

"Nee, Rose. Having a baby or not having a baby—that's something for us to dream about and pray over. It's just . . ."

Her eyes narrowed. She was fully aware he was holding something back. "Okay," she sang the word and started walking again. "Look. Grace must be too tired to walk."

The boys were helping Grace get on a sled.

"Those are some very cute and sweet kiddos," she said.

"They are. No doubt." Did Rose know how good a Mamm she was? He watched as his sons worked together to pull Grace. "If getting them to sleep early isn't easy tonight, after staying out late last night caroling and all our activities today, I'm going to put a stop to Christmas."

"Uh-huh. This from the man who starts looking forward to Christmas the first day of November."

"That's not true. I start much sooner. I just keep it to myself until it's officially November."

With the carpentry on the bedroom finished, due to the extra workers, he needed to catch up on everything else for Christmas morning. He needed to finish the children's barn and barnyard pieces, and he had yet to wrap the gifts he'd bought Rose—books for winter reading, a set of mugs with each of their names, and girly things like fancy lotion and soap from a shop that Elise had said Rose loved. He'd ordered the girly stuff online while in his office at the Hinton shop. If there was time tomorrow, he'd like to take Rose shopping for furniture for the bedroom. Was he trying to soften the blow of the annulment news he must eventually share with her? He didn't think so, but he honestly wasn't sure.

"They'll be asleep by six," Rose said. "I'm certain."

"Good thing."

"You're that far behind?"

"Ya."

She turned, walking backward. "You should've finished the bedroom weeks ago, and then you wouldn't have needed so much time on it this week."

"You're a troublemaker."

She nodded in agreement. "I am."

He pointed at the ground around her feet. "When you fall—"

"When I what?" She cupped a hand behind one ear.

"Sorry. When there's another 'gravity check,' I'll laugh, and then I'm going to shovel snow on top of you."

"You have a strange way of showing love."

"That's what my Mamm used to say." Joel smiled.

"She *used* to say it? What does she say now?"

"I'm so glad you have a home of your own."

Rose laughed and then hurried toward the porch. "Last one home gets to bring in firewood for the night."

He picked up his pace. "Brr. We're going to need a lot of wood on such a cold night."

When he reached her, she turned and pushed him back. "No way. Get."

With a few long steps, he caught her on the porch and tried to step around her, but she elbowed him back and tried to get into the house. He put his arm around her waist and hauled her toward the stacked firewood.

She kicked her feet and flailed her arms. "I'll get you for this, Joel Dienner."

"Looks to me as if you're getting wood, lots of it." They both laughed, making white puffs of their breath appear in the dusky air.

A rig pulled onto the driveway, bringing the horseplay to a stop. Joel's Daed got out of the rig and headed toward the front door of the house.

"Daed," Joel called. "Over here." He took Rose's hand, making sure she didn't slip as they made their way back to the snow-packed path.

"Oh." Daed glanced at Rose and tried unsuccessfully to shove a fat envelope into his coat pocket. *"Hallo."*

Joel suspected the envelope contained something about the annulment since Daed was trying to keep it out of Rose's sight.

"Hi." She nodded with a smile, but her eyes moved to the

envelope before she gestured toward the house. “I have a stew ready, just needs heating up. Care to join us?”

“Nee. Denki.” Daed fumbled with the envelope, still trying to get it into his pocket. It caught on the flap of his coat pocket, slipped from his fingers, and fell to the ground. When the wind grabbed it and tossed it like a tumbleweed, he gasped. “It’s information for you, Joel. Don’t let it get away.”

Rose quickly caught up to it, grabbed it, and handed it to Joel, her eyes reflecting questions she wouldn’t ask, at least not until his Daed was gone.

“Denki.” His Daed was as bumfuzzled as Joel had ever seen him. What was in the envelope? Surely not the church leaders’ decision. They had said it’d be weeks. “I need a minute with Joel, please.”

“Okay.” Rose’s eyes probed him as she passed, and he knew, Christmastime or not, avoiding this conversation had come to an end.

“Sorry,” his Daed breathed. “Could I be more obvious or make this any harder on you?”

“It’s okay, Daed. Don’t worry about it.” What else could Joel say? His Daed meant no harm.

“I copied some information on annulments at the library when your Mamm and I were in Beckley yesterday. I thought it would be helpful to have more details on the rules of the county and the state.” He passed the envelope to Joel. “I’m just trying to be helpful, Joel. I want you and Rose to be prepared when the leaders pass down their opinion about the way forward for you two."

As Joel took it, he looked toward the house and saw Rose watching him before she slipped inside and closed the door.

While the children washed up, Rose needed to begin reheating the meaty stew she had cooked earlier in the pot on the wood stove. Instead she waited at the counter, where she could keep an eye on the back door. What would cause such secrecy, such panic in her father-in-law when he dropped the envelope? Her heart thudded mercilessly against her chest.

Joel entered the house, his head ducked as he walked toward the kitchen. He handed her some wood for the stove, then laid the envelope on the counter. "We'll talk when the children are asleep."

She knew her place, and it wasn't to question or argue when the head of the home gave a decree. Getting the fire to burn hotter to reheat the stew came first. To hurry up the process of heating dinner, maybe she should pour the stew into a different pot and set it on an eye of the gas stove. But neither way seemed fast enough. Joel moved to a cabinet and pulled out bowls.

She envisioned herself watching the beef stew warm, ladling it out, and the children prattling excitedly throughout dinner. She even imagined going through the nightly routine of getting them in bed—helping them change into pajamas and brush their teeth before they snuggled on the couch and read delicious passages of fiction before finally saying their prayers and climbing into bed.

Strangely disobedient, her will felt like a feral animal, free from all control. It wouldn't cooperate with what she knew needed to happen and in what order, so she remained in place, staring at the envelope. "No."

The bowls in Joel's hand clanked, and she realized he'd almost dropped them.

She picked up the envelope. "Is this connected to whatever is distracting you?"

"I haven't been . . ." He dropped the sentence and paused before he moved his head as if he was both nodding and shaking it. "Ya."

"Joel, I'd like to know what's in it."

The children sounded like a team of sled dogs coming down the stairs, yelping and scuffling playfully. She needed to tend to them, just as she had done for four years without fail, no matter what was going on. And it was life, so there was always a measure of difficult things going on.

"What's for dinner?" Mose asked, sniffing the air. "Smells great."

Their little voices rose, asking, talking, demanding. It was enough to drown out all possibility of adult conversation.

The stew was only lukewarm, and Joel grabbed a paper grocery bag out of the drawer and went to the refrigerator. He put grapes, oranges, and their reusable water bottles into the bag. He stopped by the pantry and tossed a package of Goldfish crackers into it. "Mose, take your brother and sister upstairs to my room. Eat what's in here. Do not come down until I say you can."

Joel's room was the farthest one down the hall, so apparently he was trying to ensure they wouldn't overhear.

Mose peered into the bag. "What about dessert?"

Joel grabbed the plate of homemade gingerbread men off the counter and shoved it into the bag. He put his hand on Levi's shoulder and pointed him toward the steps. "You too. All three, upstairs."

Grace peered up at him, looking concerned.

He smiled. "Go on, baby girl. It's an indoor picnic on my sectional."

Her worry turned into excitement, and she ran up the steps behind her brothers.

The room grew quiet, and Joel pulled out a chair for her.

She shook her head. "I'm not sure I can sit. What's the bad news?"

"It's not bad news."

"Your body language says otherwise."

He nodded. "It's only bad news—bad news for me—if you think it's the best thing to ever happen to a married Amish couple."

Rose's confusion expanded. His words made no sense. "What are you talking about?"

As Joel explained, she tried to wrap her mind around the word *annulment.* She should've sat down when he suggested it, but she locked her knees, determined to stay in place. Despite his flowery words and gentle tone, she saw the truth he was dancing around. Joel had found a way to get out of being married to her.

"Rose, honey?" He tried to slip his hands into hers. "I've been very concerned how this might sound, so much so that I didn't want to talk about it until after Christmas. I need you to hear me. What the church leaders back in Pennsylvania are doing doesn't mean anything. We love you. Me, the children, and this community. We were broken, and God sent an angel to Forest Hill."

An angel. Ya, right. "An angel you needed four years ago,

and now that the children are older, this angel just isn't needed anymore, right? Especially since there's a new and attractive widow in Forest Hill."

He groaned, clearly frustrated. "Rose, could you just *try* to hear what I'm saying?"

She heard plenty. He just seemed to think she was deaf to what he wasn't saying. She pulled away, and the only thing she could think was that she finally understood what it felt like to have someone in your life one minute and then gone the next. "Now what?"

He held out the envelope. "Daed gathered information on annulments at the library in Beckley. He copied some of the documents so we'd be fully informed when the decision comes back from the leaders."

"Very noble." She took the envelope. "Of course, a more noble thing would have been if the two of you had talked with me about it on Tuesday. Why are you hiding information—from your wife and the one you professed to love?"

"I . . . Rose, the way you are responding, right now—I wanted to avoid this."

"Avoid this? You could have just put the truth out there. 'I appreciate all you've done for us, but I just found out the church might allow us to dissolve our marriage. I'm actually not in love with you after all.' "

"What?" His brows furrowed, wrinkling his forehead. "That's not what's going on here."

"I think it is. Tuesday morning you said all the right things while trying to console and calm me down when Gertie showed up gifting you with clothing she'd made. But then you learned you could have a different life. One without difficult Rose."

"That's not what was going on." He rubbed the back of his neck. "I misspoke to Erma on Monday night, and she took the news to Daed. That's why he and the preacher came here to talk to me."

Rose paused for a moment, thinking about Erma and how she treated Joel and Rose's personal information. Her skin burned as unbridled anger rose from some abandoned place inside her. "But couldn't you have told that preacher not to even consider discussing our marriage? That we'd never want an annulment and were on our way to an intimate marriage?"

He closed his eyes. "Ya, I tried but—"

"No buts, Joel. You wanted to know if our marriage could be easily voided. You didn't stop them. And you kept all of it from me while . . ." She looked at the closed bedroom doors, embarrassed at how hard she'd been pushing for them to begin a new chapter of their lives. "Forget how awful this makes me feel, how unloved and stupid. You know I want us to have a *real* married life. But why would you be willing to break up the family and wound your children?"

"I don't want the family to break up. It's hard to imagine the pain it would cause the children. Listen to me, Rose."

She shook the envelope at him. "If the marriage was dissolved, what were you thinking was going to happen to me? That I could just visit the children? I have a better plan. You move out. I'll help you pack, and I'll live here with the children."

He blinked, looking bewildered by her suggestion.

"What, Joel? You don't like it when it's your life being jerked out from under you?"

"But I'm not trying to take anything from you. This is what I was afraid of! I . . . thought—"

"Ya, I know what you're thinking. They're *your* children. You remind me and them of that whenever you're annoyed with me." Still holding the envelope in one hand, she fisted the other. "I hate when you call me *stepmom*. Why do you do that? We are very open with the children about who their real Mamm is. We have them call me Mama to make sure I'm not infringing on her place. We talk of her to them. So tell me, why remind them that I'm a stepmom?"

He appeared surprised by the territory the argument had entered, and it took him a moment to answer. "Sometimes I feel they need a reminder that you don't owe them every breath you take. You've been a great gift to all of us—but at the cost of your own interests and identity."

"I set good boundaries."

"Sometimes. At other times you give them too much of your day and energy."

"They're children. I'm the only mother they have now, and it's what a mom does. This annulment isn't about the church's concerns with our marriage. You're just looking for a dash toward freedom."

"Rose, you're letting your imagination be fueled by old pain. I get how I've set a brush fire." He shook his head, clearly distraught. "It's what I feared most—that this thing from out of nowhere would fan flames of doubt. How you feel right now isn't based on what's happening today or this week. Listen to me. I was so caught off guard and offended that I didn't gather my wits and argue with the preacher, and that was wrong. But remember that I started the addition of the bedroom. Can't you hear me when I say I love you?"

"No, I can't. Not at this point. I heard you when you said it on Tuesday. Since then I've been the one asking for every kiss, and I asked the men to help finish our bedroom. And you? You started keeping a pretty important secret." She shoved the envelope into the hidden pocket of her apron. "Now when you tell me how you feel, I can't be as quick to believe you. I need some fresh air." She grabbed her coat and went outside.

Night had fallen, and the darkness pressed in hard. She went to the barn, lit a lantern, and hitched the horse to the carriage. Holding tight to the leather reins, she pulled out of the driveway. In her four years of living here, had she once left the house by herself? Whenever she left without any of the children, she was with Joel.

Her thoughts were as scattered as her heart was broken. She could deal with being a second-class wife. As things go, she had been dealt a very good hand—a fun and kind husband, three sweet and smart-as-a-whip children, a lovely home, a comfortable income, a supportive community, and a few really good friends—like Elise, Shirley Wagner, and Joel's Mamm, Sarah. But to be uncertain that he ever would or could love her?

Tension made her shoulders ache, and her knuckles were white from gripping the reins. The *clippety-clop* of the horse's hoofs against the cold pavement worked some of the angst out of her shoulders. Why would Erma start this kind of trouble between Joel and her? The woman didn't like her, but did she know the irreversible damage she'd done? Rose and Joel had come so far, respecting and trusting each other all along the way.

When Erma's house came into sight, Rose was tempted to stop there.

"Just stay on the road," she mumbled, but despite herself she pulled onto the driveway. What was she doing here? Some people could be reasoned with. From all Rose had seen, Erma was not one of them. Still, she tethered the horse to the hitching post, went to the front door, and knocked.

Leo, Erma's better half, opened the door. The old man's eyes grew as big as his smile. "Hey, Rose, kumm." He peered out the door. "Are you by yourself?"

"I am."

Either she or Joel brought the children here two or three times a month and stayed to help while the little ones visited their grandparents. Maybe part of Rose's anger was that she'd gone out of her way to treat Erma fairly. Was Leo in agreement with Erma, disliking Rose and willing to meddle? It didn't seem as if he was against her. He responded as warm as sunshine to her, had since her first month here.

"Leo?" Erma called. "Who's here?"

He motioned for Rose to follow him. "Rose is. She's by herself."

They went into the living room, where Erma was rocked back in the recliner with a pillow under her knees and one under each elbow. Her ankles and the joints in her hands were quite swollen. Erma stared at her.

Rose took a seat on the couch. Her heart raced, but now that she was facing Erma, she knew what she wanted to say. She had a story to share, one she'd never told anyone for fear of being accused of witchcraft. She no longer cared. "It might sound like deviltry, but in early December four years ago, the same week that Joel returned to work after taking two months off, Mose and Levi contracted the flu. I'd taken them to the doctor's and had meds and instructions, but I couldn't get Levi's fever down, and I couldn't get him to drink anything. I was starting to panic. I didn't know Joel well, and I was afraid he'd be angry if I called him home on his second day back. I was terrified for little Levi. What if I handled the situation wrong and he died? All three children were whiny or crying, and I couldn't think clearly to save my life. I remember standing in the kitchen, paralyzed with fear, asking, what do I need to do? Sometimes I pray these words: 'Dear God, if it's not a bother, show me what to do, and let Your truth set me free.' Is that silly? But peace came from nowhere and encircled me. And just like the night I arrived and knew what I needed to do about getting breast milk for Grace, I knew what I needed to do for Levi. It was as if Florence was right there with me, guiding me. I went to the closet in Joel's bedroom office, a place I'd never gone to before, and I pulled out an adult-sized tea set. I steeped tea and added ice cubes, and I took it to the bathroom, where I fixed a lukewarm bubble bath and got Levi and Mose in the tub. We played high tea, and he drank every bit of the liquid. He then drank cool tap water directly from the teapot. There was no way I knew where that tea set was or that Levi would take in liquid while he was in a tub."

"That's not deviltry. That's God," Leo said. "And maybe somehow it was Florence."

Rose put her arms on her thighs and leaned forward.

"Sometimes when I least expect it, it's as if I can hear her whisper, 'Denki, Rose. Denki.' "

One thing was for sure, despite the overwrought emotions of the last few weeks, Rose wasn't the same young woman who'd arrived four years ago. That person couldn't have stood up for herself. As much as she'd given Joel, he'd given back to her—drop by kind drop.

Erma stared straight ahead as if the bookcase held a television showing something mesmerizing.

"That's nice," Leo said. "None of us knows God's ways of leading us. If Florence can see you, I imagine she is saying, 'Thank you.' "

Rose was aware how very dry her mouth felt. "But I know if she can see me and if she's whispered thanks, it's not about what I got right. The whispers are because my heart is set on doing as much right by her children and Joel as I possibly can." Rose stood, focused on Erma. "If Florence whispered to you, what would she say?" She moved to the side of Erma's chair and whispered in her ear, "I think she'd ask, 'What are you doing, Mamm? Is *your* heart set on doing right?' "

Erma's eyes never left the wall. "You need to leave."

"Did you stir a stink, Erma?" Leo angled his head. "I've told you a hundred times to leave Rose and Joel alone."

Rose's eyes misted, and she kissed Leo's cheek. "Denki."

"Don't let anything come between you and Joel."

She wanted to tell him it was too late for that. Erma had wanted to hurt and embarrass her. She'd wanted to come between Joel and her and ruin their camaraderie and trust. The woman had accomplished her goal.

But Rose just nodded and slipped out the door.

Joel had turned the kerosene lamps as high as they could go, and one of the two portable gas pole lights sputtered as the propane tank threatened to run out of fuel. It was two in the morning, and Rose was still out for some *fresh air.* His blood was simmering as he turned the flathead screwdriver, attaching the brackets for the curtain rod. The new bedroom echoed with each move he made, a sure sign that the furniture, bedding, and rugs were missing. That might have something to do with the fact that he and Rose hadn't shopped for any of it yet. Would they ever?

Cold air seeped through the window he'd opened a few inches so he could hear her carriage when she returned. His best guess was that she was at Elise's, safe and sound. He'd like to confirm that, but he refused to call—maybe because he wanted to respect her right for space or maybe because he was too angry to chase after her. He knew that much of his anger was at himself because she had responded to the annulment conversation as badly as he'd worried she might, and he hadn't handled it well.

The distant *clippety-clops* of a horse's hoofs on pavement caught his attention, and he got off the stepladder and went out on the front porch. Warm peace and agitation flooded him when the rig turned onto the driveway. It was Rose, and she was safe. She went right past him and pulled into the barn. He stepped back into the house and grabbed his coat.

It was now December 23, just two days before Christmas, and not only had the past several hours been completely frustrating, but he doubted things would improve anytime soon. Both he and Rose were in limbo. They didn't have to be. She could choose to believe he loved her and say she wasn't interested in whether an annulment was possible. But no.

"Women," he mumbled as he strode toward the barn.

In this moment some of the traditions of his faith struck him as unfair. Women were smart and emotionally wise, but Amish men were supposed to be the leaders at all times. As if his gender automatically made him better at knowing what to do in every situation. Clearly it didn't.

The silvery glow of the moon against the snow illuminated the night, and Rose was a mere silhouette inside the barn as she got out of the rig. She lit a kerosene lantern. Her hair was down, and the prayer Kapp was in her hand. She looked weary and disheveled and completely unaware of him.

He paused just inside the building. "Hey." His voice was a low rumble through the barn.

She glanced up. "Hi." She began removing the rigging from the horse, and he disconnected the carriage and rolled it out of the way.

Maybe he should've gone to her with the information about the annulment on Tuesday. Clearly he'd spared neither of them anything by doing it his way. It was part of his natural design to pick the right moment for a big conversation. He and Rose had successfully navigated four years by that method, these past weeks excluded, as the right moment to talk about his vision for the new room hadn't presented itself either. He sighed and thought maybe it was time to change how he communicated with his wife.

"I'm going to bed." She dug the envelope out of her coat pocket, laid it on a hay bale, and walked toward the double-wide doorway of the barn.

"Rose, wait."

She paused and turned. "I'm exhausted, Joel."

If she could really hear him for two minutes, they could clear the air. But since she was hurt, all she heard when he spoke was her Mamm's belittling. She couldn't believe he valued her because she couldn't see her value. He imagined it would be like looking into a mirror but seeing a raccoon staring back at him. If her Mamm hadn't been a raging backbiter, maybe Rose could see herself for who she was. And not turn the whole thing upside down.

He picked up the envelope. "I've insulted and offended you, but can you give me a break here? This whole mess hit like a tornado, with no time for me to think. I made a bad call. But—"

"Ya." She held up one hand. "I got it. Elise says you're right and I'm wrong."

The muscles throughout his body tightened. If she hadn't believed Elise on matters of husbands and wives and love, he had little chance that she'd hear him. "My actions weren't perfect, but they didn't convey what you think."

"Maybe." She nodded and said nothing else for several long moments. "That's the problem. However I look at this, the best I can come up with is maybe you weren't looking for a way out. And that's not good enough. Not for a real marriage, it isn't." She shook her head. "I've decided that I need to go home, to my parents' house, for a bit. I haven't been back since arriving here four years ago, and now seems like the perfect time. I need more than a few hours away, Joel." She sighed. "Elise is picking up Grace and me this morning after the boys go to school."

"For how long?"

"I'm not sure. A couple of days, I think." She walked toward the house.

Did she intend to stay through Christmas? Through New Year's Day? He decided to leave those decisions up to her without asking questions.

"If that's what you need, then I'm for it, but I need you to know that I believe all marriages have their own story. One where you love so much it makes your head spin. When your heart isn't soaring with delight, it aches with shared grief. It's a union so strong you'd do anything for your spouse, the very one who can anger you more than anyone. But that person owns half of you, and the love between the two of you is stronger than any anger." He watched the snowflakes whirl around her, wishing she'd face him. "Rose, I'm head over heels in love with you."

She turned toward him again, blank faced as she stood in the falling snow watching him. The moon caressed her body and long flowing hair. She looked like the angel he thought her to be. In the Old Testament, Jacob wrestled with an angel, so clearly angels were fierce too.

She drew a deep breath. "Ya, maybe so."

She went toward the house, leaving him in the cold.

15

As Elise pulled her Yukon to the side of the old farmhouse, Rose glanced at the clock on the dashboard. Almost one thirty in the afternoon. They had made good time. Elise turned off the SUV, but Rose remained in place, studying the house she'd grown up in. It seemed odd how little she'd missed this place.

Elise unbuckled her seat belt. "You need a minute?"

"No. I'm fine." Rose's heart pounded as she got out of the vehicle and opened the door to the backseat. "You ready to stretch those legs, sweetheart?"

"Ya, Mama. But let me do it."

"Okay." Rose prepared to wait a minute. The *it* was unbuckling the harness and buckle connector to her car seat.

Elise came around the vehicle. “Should I get your overnight bag now?”

“Not yet. Let’s see how the afternoon goes. Okay?”

Elise nodded. “Good thinking.”

During the long trip here, Rose could’ve clarified a few things about her plans, but she hadn’t felt like talking.

Once Grace was free of her car-seat restraints, she held her arms toward her mama. Rose lifted her out and held her.

The side door of the old farmhouse opened, and Rose’s Mamm stepped out, using one hand to shield her eyes from the sun to see who was in her driveway.

Maybe Rose should’ve called before arriving. “Hi, Mamm. It’s me.” Rose walked toward her but stopped a few feet away.

Mamm lowered her hand, clearly able to see Rose now, but she just stood there.

“Mamm, this is Grace. Grace, this is your *Mammi* Kate.”

Grace held out her hand. “Pleased to meet you.”

The sternness on Mamm’s face eased a bit. “She knows a lot of Englisch for a girl her age.”

Grace’s skill in both languages at this age was intentional on Rose’s part, but she knew her Mamm wouldn’t see it as a good thing.

Rose drew a deep breath and stepped closer. “You should shake her hand, Mamm.”

Mamm shook her hand. "I suppose I'm pleased to meet you too."

Rose knew what her Mamm meant. She wouldn't truly know if she was pleased until she got to know the little girl a bit.

"I gotta go potty."

"Oh." Mamm chuckled. "That's quite direct, isn't it? I like that." She motioned. "Kumm."

Grace wriggled to get down and trotted behind as Mamm led the way.

Elise stepped next to Rose. "Wow. I'm not sure what I expected, but it wasn't that. This fills in a lot of blanks about how you respond to things. We could stay for an hour and head home."

"I have to stay for a little while, more than an hour, I think. I want to be different, Elise, to stop seeing myself the way I do. Whenever a problem needs to be worked out, her voice is louder than any others, telling me how I messed up everything. It's not real, it's not happening now, but I can't hear anything else, and it's threatening to ruin my marriage." Rose paused. "Besides, in Mamm's eyes what I did was find a church-approved way of leaving her on this dairy farm with my Daed, eleven brothers, and an unbearable amount of chores to do each day, so don't judge her reaction too harshly."

Elise's brows furrowed into a V. "She sees you for the first time in more than four years, and she didn't even hug you."

"I didn't think she would, even if she wanted to."

"Yeah, well, I packed a bag too just in case you needed me, and I think you do. If you stay the night, I stay. If you don't mind. I can head home in the morning. With Gigi and Pap visiting, my kids won't even notice I'm not there."

"Thank you." Rose was grateful to have a friend who cared so much. She went inside and held the door for Elise.

Mamm stood at the sink, adding water to the kettle.

"Mamm, this is my friend Elise."

Mamm looked at her and nodded. "I'm Kate." She turned off the water. "Either of you care for some tea?"

"Ya. Denki." Rose sat on a barstool at the island, and she gestured for Elise to do the same. Rose looked around the room. "You have new cabinets."

"No. I sanded them and added some fresh paint. I wish I'd left well enough alone, but the damage is done."

Grace came out of the bathroom and climbed in Rose's lap. Rose kissed her head. "Would you like some tea?"

Grace nodded. "With sugar and cream, right, Mama?"

"Ya, of course." When Grace was given tea, which wasn't often, she liked more sugar and cream than tea.

Grace folded her little hands and put them on the island. "Okay, Mammi Kate, let's talk. What's your favorite game?"

Mamm's eyes grew large, and she smiled before glancing at Rose. "Oh, I'm way too old for games. What's yours?"

"Poons."

Mamm looked at Rose, clearly hoping for a bit of help.

"Spoons," Rose said. "The card game where there is one less spoon on the table than there are people playing. The boys and I used to play it." The "boys" were Rose's eleven brothers.

"But"—Grace wagged her finger—"you gotta grab the s-spoon fast, or they'll disappear off the table." Grace spread her arms out. "Poof. All gone. Too bad. So sad."

Mamm broke into laughter. "Well, you're just a card yourself, aren't you?"

"Daed says I'm me, but I also take after both my Mamm *and* my Mama, and he says that's the best recipe ever." She nodded. "Yep. That's what he says."

Mamm's brows knit as her eyes searched Rose's, and then she turned her attention back to Grace. "Do you know what I have?" Mamm asked while walking to the window seat. She lifted the lid and pulled out an old faceless cloth doll that had belonged to Rose and slid it across the island to Grace.

"Look, Mama." Grace held it up. "She's missing her eyes, nose, and mouth, but she's got ears. Why's that?"

"It's called a faceless doll, and it's just the way dolls were in this house, Grace." Rose hadn't ever felt as if she were missing her eyes, but she'd been keenly aware that she was supposed to listen with her ears and keep her mouth shut. An old dream she used to have came back to her, one where her jaws were wired shut.

"Kumm." Mamm motioned to Grace. "There are a few other toys in here too."

Grace wriggled down, leaving the doll there. She knelt in front of the window seat and pulled out a spinning top, plastic plates and utensils, and doll furniture. Memories of sitting right where Grace was came back to Rose—the carefree days before she turned six or seven and Mamm expected her to do the work of someone twice her age and with the same expertise. By the age of twelve, Rose was always in trouble for not doing flawless work, work that she now knew would take two women. And who did flawless work? Certainly not Rose.

Rose caressed the doll's head and arms as her Mamm set out mugs, added tea bags, and poured in hot water. Ears to hear and hands to work—that's all a girl needed in this house.

Mamm set a cup in front of Elise first and then Rose. "Your Daed and brothers are out preparing their stands for deer season. It opens in three days, you know. But they'll be home in time for dinner and milking. Will you stay that long?"

Was that a bit of hope in her Mamm's voice?

"Sure, Mamm."

"Gut. Daed and the boys will be pleased."

"All of them? None of my brothers is married yet?" One

brother was a year older than she was, and the rest were younger, but three of them were of marrying age now. Mamm's few letters each year had consisted of the weather, the production of the milk cows, and whose health was improving or waning in the family and church.

Mamm gave a look that almost resembled rolling her eyes. "Not yet. Not even a steady girl for any of them."

That was interesting, and Rose wondered if her difficult Mamm had deterred all prospects.

"What can Elise and I do to help get dinner on the table?"

"Oh." Mamm's brows went up, and she seemed excited. "You know, I have a side of smoked ham, and the boys would love to have your ham surprise special."

Rose had never thought to write down the few recipes she'd devised that her brothers loved. So she wasn't surprised that the dishes hadn't made the supper rotation.

"She's made that for my family a few times too. We love it," Elise said.

Mamm's excitement dimmed. "On second thought, aside from the ham, I doubt I have all you'd need for that recipe."

"Pffft." Elise made a shooing motion with one hand. "I have a car. I can get to the store and back with the right stuff before Rose has the ham chopped for sautéing."

While Rose's Mamm and Elise chatted, Rose began making homemade pasta to go in her concoction. Grace climbed up and down on the barstool at will, sipping her tea and then returning to the box to play with the toys. None of it seemed to grate on Mamm's nerves. Actually, she seemed to enjoy watching Grace, which was not how Rose remembered her childhood. Elise ran to the store and back.

Three hours flew by swiftly, and with a loud thud her oldest brother walked into the house. "Rose?" He blinked. "Well, you do still exist. I'd heard rumors about it." He grinned before awkwardly hugging her. Soon there was a stampede of men and half-grown men greeting her. Most just smiled and spoke, but a few hugged her, as did her Daed. Before long they were seated at the table.

Her chair, the one she'd sat in most of her life, seemed to whisper memories to her, and she was surprised to recall many enjoyable ones. It was in this chair she'd received one birthday present each year. This chair is where she sat to play board games with her brothers during the long winters. This chair had been her friend when she was hungry and tired, but there were plenty of mealtimes when she hardly sat for helping to serve her brothers and Daed. Her Mamm used to fuss over every little thing—like the way the chair scraped against the floor when Rose got up or how slowly she moved to get another container of butter, even though in Rose's opinion she'd been sprinting.

"How long are you staying, Rose?" Daed asked. Her feelings about her Daed were mixed. He wasn't as hard on her as her Mamm was, but she never remembered a time when he came to her defense.

She didn't have a good answer for him. "At least until the supper dishes are done."

"That long." He chuckled. "What's Forest Hill like?"

She started describing her life now, and the conversation was comfortable and easy as her brothers asked questions and shared what they knew about lakes and canoes and tourist seasons. Her seventeen-year-old brother, Matt, showed real interest in Joel's business, digging into the details Rose provided.

Elise talked as much as anyone else, and Grace ate well while entertaining her uncles with her lengthy explanations about anything they dared to ask. The visit felt like a victory, even if she and her Mamm never showed any warm affection toward each other.

"That was a great meal, Rose." Her eldest brother stood. "But the cows won't milk themselves. Games after?"

Her brothers had never been particularly kind. Most often they ignored her or treated her like a servant, but they had also enjoyed some good times. "I'd like that."

Chairs squawked against the cheap vinyl flooring as all the men left the house. Elise took Grace to see how a large herd of cows was milked compared to the way they milked Clarabelle by hand.

Rose stood and began helping her Mamm clean up, unsure what else they could make small talk about.

Mamm shoved scraps off one plate and onto another. "I have a girl coming to help most days but not this week since it's so close to Christmas and all."

"That's great . . . about the help. I know it had to be hard—me leaving the way I did."

Mamm nodded. "Ya. It was." She took a stack of dishes to the sink and filled the basin with water, adding a good squirt of dish detergent.

Rose brought another stack. "So how many horses do the boys have now?"

Her Mamm started to take the plates from her, but when their eyes met, she held Rose's gaze without moving. "I can't do this. I can't chitchat about unimportant things while we ignore the elephant in the room." She took the dishes and put them on the counter, grabbed Rose by the wrist, and walked to the living room. "Sit." She motioned across the room with its many chairs. "Somewhere."

Rose moved to her old spot on the end of the couch that was closest to the fireplace.

Mamm sat in her rocker. "I need to say some things. It shouldn't take more than fifteen minutes. Can you deal with that?"

"I . . . think so."

"Gut. When you left, it was hard. Really hard, and I was furious with you. I hired one girl after another, but none of them, not even three at a time, were enough help. They were untrained and lazy, every one of them. So I went to the bishop to tell him how wrong he'd been to agree to your marriage, leaving us here without anyone."

"Mamm." Rose gasped. "You didn't."

"I did. I was too angry not to. I told him he'd given you an easy way out of staying where God put you, and you took it. He looked me square in the eyes and asked, 'Do you blame her?' " Mamm slapped her palms against the wooden armrests. "Then he said all sorts of other things I didn't know he knew. Some I hadn't remembered—like saying that from the time you were little, people could hear me yelling at you, calling you names, from far and wide. And he said I was the problem." She pointed at herself. "Of course, I didn't believe him. I had no recollection of calling you names, not for a while anyway. But life piled on the pressure back then when I had all these little boys, and, yes, I was angry. Still, I wasn't the woman he described, was I? Cruel? After fuming for weeks, I got what I thought was a second letter from you, and I was sure you'd written to tell me how sorry you were—you know, 'cause I pointed out all you'd done wrong over the years in my previous letter. Telling how you let me down. But the letter wasn't from you. It was from Joel. We both know what that letter said." Mamm took a breath. "He was respectful, even kind, but he didn't let anything I'd written slide by without addressing it, and I had to look at the truth. It took me a little while to see it. In my exhaustion and irritability, I'd been a mean Mamm to you, and I had to live with it." Mamm shook a finger at her. "You're a good girl with a lot of wonderful qualities. You know that, right?"

Rose could hardly speak. "Denki, Mamm."

Mamm rocked back and forth while Rose gained her composure. "But, Mamm, you never wrote me about any of this. The letters . . . You never shared your heart before."

"I tried to write the words or say them on the phone. I couldn't. Now, looking you in the eyes tonight, seeing the sweet bond between you and Grace, and knowing I wrecked what we should have, I couldn't hold back what needed to be said. Your Daed is real sorry too. It keeps him up at night, but he won't share his regrets with anyone except me." She clutched the wooden armrests, looking rather stern. "Is Joel good to you? His letter seemed as if he would be, but please tell me I didn't run you off and into the arms of a bad husband."

"No, Mamm. He's a really good husband. Maybe the best ever, but things have changed recently, and I don't know what to do about it."

"You want to tell me?" Mamm's eyes looked wet. "I want to do better by you, Rose."

Her words melted Rose's heart, and she opened up about her marriage, probably telling way too much.

"That explains why you haven't conceived yet." Mamm smiled. "Do you love him?"

In her former days Mamm would've scolded Rose for not consummating the vows and would've told her she was an embarrassment to the family. Her Mamm had changed.

"Ya, Mamm, I do love him. I never imagined love like this existed."

"You go home to him, Rose. Tomorrow is Christmas Eve, and you should be with your husband and children. It doesn't matter if everything feels shattered. If you're broken but together, you can mend together. That's how it works." Mamm got up and went into her bedroom. When she returned, she walked over to Rose and pressed a small stack of folded money into her hand. "That's so you can hire a driver and come for a longer visit when it's convenient. Bring all my grandbabies, okay?"

"Ya." She took the money, knowing her Mamm needed her to accept the gift. She stood and hugged her. "Denki, Mamm."

Mamm hugged her for a few long seconds before backing away. "Goodness. All this tenderness. Why, my Mamm would roll over in her grave, and if our men saw it, they would laugh us right out of this house." She straightened her apron. "Dishes." She pointed at the sink. "Now."

Rose smiled and went to the sink. The evening floated by, and talking with her brothers came easily. Rose excused herself long enough to tuck Grace into bed, and Elise went to bed too. Rose went downstairs again and won several rounds of Dutch Blitz against her brothers before they turned in, content to get only a few hours of sleep before the early-morning milking. When Rose crawled into bed next to Grace, she snuggled with her girl. She was ready to go back home, even if she didn't know how Joel really felt toward her. After all, he was a kind, good man who'd been trapped into marrying her. His kindness alone could be the cause of his being less than honest with her.

But what if he did mean what he'd said?

Hope stirred within her. She wouldn't really know how he felt until she could accept herself and believe she was worthy of his love. It seemed impossible for her to get to that place, but her Mamm's attitude had changed considerably when she was confronted by the truth. Rose needed to see the truth too.

But how?

Rose stood between the barn and the house, holding Grace's hand and waving as Elise pulled out of the driveway. The midmorning light was gray as snow flurries swirled. They had left Rose's parents' house a little after four in the morning, about the same time the menfolk started the milking.

It had been a better visit with her family than she could've ever hoped for, and yet she still was nervous about going inside and facing Joel.

With her overnight bag on her shoulder and Grace by the hand, she meandered into the barn. The aroma of hay, livestock, and fresh snow filled her senses. Grace filled a scoop with oats, went to the gate of the closest stall, and held it out to the horse.

Clarabelle didn't look as if she'd been milked yet, so Rose grabbed a milking stool and pail. Her insides were tied in knots, and her eyes burned from a heavy crying bout before their drive this morning. She wasn't one to cry, hadn't cried since she was a teen, but her emotions seemed short-circuited.

With her hands clasped around the cow's teats, she milked Clarabelle. Rose watched streams of warm milk hit inside the pail of white liquid, causing the surface of the liquid to shudder.

Some of the tears were because of her Mamm's unexpected kindness, but the rest were because she had been so close to having a real marriage—and then was unsure of Joel's true feelings. He'd married her because he needed a mother for his children, and now he had hidden the annulment conversation. Why?

Melancholy had taken up residence inside her and had evicted contentment. Even a trip home and a sincere apology from her Mamm couldn't make the sadness go away. It was nice that her Mamm understood now, but what Rose longed for was Joel's love—or, if it existed, to be able to believe in it.

She stopped milking and leaned her forehead against the side of the cow. "What happened, Clarabelle?" She patted her flank. "We loved this life, all of it."

Clarabelle turned, craning her neck to see Rose.

"Ya, I know," she told Clarabelle. "I'm the problem child

here. Why can't life and love be simple?" She set the full pail to the side and put the stool back in its place before stepping in front of Clarabelle and rubbing her head. "When I started caring for Joel differently but he didn't seem to feel the same way, I consoled myself that no matter what we'd be together—with a bonded, lasting friendship-type marriage—even if we were in separate bedrooms for another decade."

A door slammed, and she knew someone had come out of the house. She gave Clarabelle a final nuzzle, grabbed the pail, and left the stall. "Grace, it's time to go in."

Grace threw the plastic scoop toward the oat bin, and it hit the ground as she hurried out of the barn. Rose didn't have it in her to remind Grace to put it where it belonged.

Walking out of the barn, Rose saw Joel at the woodpile, filling his arms with wood for the fireplace and stove. Snow swirled about, and she longed to hurry toward him and chat as if everything was back to normal. She drew a breath and headed for the house instead.

"Daed!" Grace ran for him as if they'd been separated for weeks.

Joel shifted the stack of wood to one arm and knelt. Grace hugged him with both arms, and he hugged her tight. He gazed up at Rose, but she pretended not to notice, looking at the milk in the pail, at the pasture, and even at the back of Grace's prayer Kapp.

"We had the best time, Daed! Mammi Kate gave me a faceless doll that belonged to Mama!" Grace kissed his cheek. "It's packed in our suitcase, but Elise said you gotta build a shelf for it 'cause if I don't play with it, I can put it up high and pass it on to my daughter one day."

He studied her. "That's great, sweetie."

Grace nodded. "I'm going to tell the boys. That's what Mama calls her brothers—the boys." Grace hurried up the stairs to the house.

Joel stood and shifted the stack of wood. Their eyes met, and his lips curved in a smile, but it didn't radiate from his eyes. What had she done? It was Christmas Eve, and they were miserable.

He nodded. "Morning. I'm glad you're back."

"Hi, yeah." She forced her feet to move, and she went up the stairs and into the house ahead of him. The aroma of coffee filled the air. He'd fed the boys and had a roaring fire going, and she had milked the cow. They were a good team.

She went into the kitchen and he into the living room. While she stored milk in containers and put them in the fridge, Joel continued bringing in wood and filling the woodbins.

She put his favorite snack on to bake—coffeecake made from an instant-potato starter. Joel went outside again, and a few minutes later returned with the newspaper. She poured him a cup of coffee and set it at his spot.

"Denki." He smiled again, clearly trying to be friendly. The chair at the head of the table squeaked as he shifted it to sit down. "Rose, when you want to talk about your trip, I'm very interested in hearing about it."

She felt her chest tighten. Could she tell him what happened with her Mamm? "Okay . . . it was good. But not yet."

He nodded and then began reading his paper, and she returned to her kitchen duties. Today was about just the five of them—their favorite foods and activities. Christmas Day was for extended family, which was Joel's parents, siblings, and cousins. Second Christmas, which took place on the twenty-sixth, was about spending time with distant family and close friends.

She would call her parents and brothers tomorrow, but they might have even less to say than usual since she had just been with them. Her mind unintentionally drifted to a Christmas when she was much younger, when her mother's anger was constant. The pain of those awful days flooded her, and she realized it was a very familiar pain—the same one she was feeling with Joel.

Dear God, I've wasted too much of my life undermining myself and doubting my worthiness. I'm so weary of feeling unloved. I don't care if I'm this way because of the damage done as I grew up. I need Your help to get free.

She couldn't determine what Joel's motivations were regarding the annulment if all she could see and feel was her unworthiness. She was addicted to thoughts of being unloved and unworthy. That part of who she was had stayed relatively hidden until she became vulnerable in front of Joel.

Let Your truth set me free.

Since arriving in Forest Hill, she had been set free in a lot of ways. Joel was more than kind and patient. He believed in her in ways she never believed in herself. She couldn't ask to live in a better home.

Fresh hurt rolled through her, but she pushed it aside and sat in her spot adjacent to his. She fought with herself, wanting to put her hand over his, but she just couldn't. There had been too much rejection from him for her to reach out again.

He set the folded newspaper aside, his eyes searching hers. *"Frehlich Grischtdaag, mei sweet, Rose."* The tenderness in his voice made tears well in her eyes.

Her heart moved to her throat, and she clutched his hand, wanting to wish him a Merry Christmas too, but the words wouldn't come.

He ran his fingers over her hand. "How about we set aside the disagreements and angst and enjoy Christmas?"

She nodded. "Denki."

"If I can be out of the doghouse for at least three days, you don't need to thank me. I thank you." He held up his mug as if cheering her.

Was he telling her the truth—that he loved her?

The next hours became a dance of awkward silences between them. She tried to hide in the kitchen and keep him out of it. He played board games with the children in front of the fire, and she started preparations for everyone's favorite dishes for their Christmas Eve feast.

"Rose?" Joel walked into the kitchen, Levi by his side, and both had game pieces of some sort in their hands. "I think we should go ice-skating now. If we wait until our usual time, the snow will be too thick."

She wasn't sure she was up for it. Could she act like the happy mother while searching for what was true about their life together?

"You take them."

"Without you?" He looked as hurt as he was surprised. "But we always . . ." He sighed. "Your call." He turned to Levi. "Tell Grace and Mose to get dressed for ice-skating."

"Without you, Mama?" Levi seemed every bit as disappointed as his Daed.

Rose touched the tip of his nose. "You gotta cut me some slack here, kiddo. Talk Mose and Grace into accepting it too. I got a late start on this year's Christmas Eve feast, okay?" She usually baked the whole day before Christmas Eve, and she hadn't been here to do that, so her words were true. But if she felt more like herself, she'd cut even more items from tonight's menu and go skating.

"Okay, Mama. But just this one time." Levi ran off, whooping about going skating.

The frenzy of getting ready began, and the house rumbled with the pitter-patter of excited horses, a team of them. What was wrong with her? Why couldn't she stop believing in her lack of worth and believe Joel? The least she could do was pretend to believe, even if she stayed knotted up inside with doubt. That way they could continue with some shred of normalcy.

Soon Joel and the children were out the door, and she waved to the children before returning to the kitchen. This was how quiet life would be if she moved out . . . and when Grace went to school in two years. Rose longed for another baby, but more than that she just wanted to be Joel's wife the way husbands and wives were meant to be together.

As she was kneading her batch of yeast rolls, there was a loud knock on the door. Wiping her hands on a wet rag, she went to the door and opened it.

Erma?

She looked . . . different. Rose took a step back, and Erma entered. The woman reminded Rose of her Mamm. Even knowing how her Mamm had changed, Rose was damaged inside, and forgiving people for the harm they'd done didn't erase the scars. If Hank had scratched Grace's eyes, forgiving his owners wouldn't have undone the damage.

Erma unbuttoned her coat. "After you left the other night,

I went to Florence's old room. I spent hours rummaging through her things, like I do from time to time. I spent most of yesterday doing the same, and then I found something I don't recall ever seeing before." She pulled a manila envelope out from the safety of the bib of her apron and gave it to Rose. "My Florence drew this. I wanted to hold it close and feel her presence—something special for me—but I didn't feel that." She tapped the envelope. "I felt a specialness from her toward you. Just as sure as I know my name, I know she wanted you to have this."

Rose started to open the envelope, but Erma stopped her. "I need to go. I have been wrong, Rose." Erma got to the door. "It wasn't you that I hated. It just looked and felt that way to both of us, and I'm sorry." She left.

Erma's words went round and round inside Rose. "It wasn't me that Erma hated. It just looked and felt like it," Rose whispered, pondering the newness of the thought, and her world trembled as warm light seemed to penetrate the coldness of her childhood.

Her mother hadn't been angry and disappointed *in Rose* all those times. It just looked and felt that way to both Mamm and Rose.

A moment later beautiful, powerful thoughts welled within her, and she imagined God's hand reaching down and removing her from the path of her Mamm's anger and then Jesus stepping in Rose's place. Chills covered Rose from head to toe. He lifted His head and arms, looking at Rose's Mamm, and absorbed all the hurt for Rose.

She also realized what her Mamm had meant yesterday—that the harsh words weren't about her. It had just felt that way. Since the before-dawn moment when she'd seen Joel with Gertie and then learned that an annulment was being discussed, Rose had been pounded by the familiar wounds from her childhood. The rejection, the hurt, and the words of love without being able to see the truth in them—they'd ripped at her without reprieve, just as they had done before she'd moved here.

She did it to Me, Rose. Not you.

Was Rose imagining those words? They came with such power and filled her with peace. The pain of her childhood wasn't hers to bear anymore. Whenever hurtful, embarrassing words squeezed in from the past, Rose would visualize Jesus standing there in her stead.

Her hands trembled as she opened the envelope. She pulled out a thick piece of paper that had a rectangular box centered in the middle of the page with script inside it.

Believe in yourself. God does.

Rose gasped for air and had to sit down. She stumbled into a kitchen chair and read the words again.

Believe in yourself. God does.

She clutched the paper to her chest and closed her eyes, keenly aware that confidence and a sense of worthiness were being poured into her, like hot wax into a candle mold. *"Denki, Gott,"* she whispered over and over again.

The desire to look at the words again caused her to lower the paper, and she noticed the paper was filled with colored-pencil drawings of dozens of roses in an array of beautiful shades. Some of the roses had stems that wove around the words—*Believe in yourself. God does.*

Without any doubt she believed God wanted her to weave her life around those words.

She ran her fingers over the beautiful artwork. This needed to be framed and hung where Florence's children could see it every day. Her emotions were running wild and were deeply connected with God, but her thoughts turned to Joel.

The poor man. She'd been so hard on him of late. He couldn't say or do anything right because of the pain she carried that had nothing to do with him. She closed her eyes. "Denki, Gott," she whispered a dozen times. "Show me what to do right now, and let Your truth set our marriage free."

The house was filled with delicious smells as Joel ushered the children in from the cold. Grace was in his arms, holding the still-broken clock. This beautiful old timepiece needed a true clocksmith to repair it, and he would find a good one next week, but the fact that it was broken no longer bothered him. It was just an eerie coincidence that it had stopped on the two overwhelming occasions. Nothing more. But the broken heirloom had served as a good reminder that even though clocks stopped, time never stood still. With every passing minute and hour, he intended to love Rose the way she needed him to—whether or not she could believe that's how he really felt.

He took the clock from Grace's arms and set it on the

entryway cubby shelf. Grace wriggled down. He'd kept the children out as long as he could, letting them play in his shop after it got too snowy and cold to enjoy ice-skating. His hope had been to give Rose as much time as possible without them underfoot. Maybe she had even rested for a bit.

But now the children were hungry and grumpy.

"Mama!" Levi called.

Rose came out of the kitchen, a welcoming smile on her face. Her eyes moved to Joel's, and she smiled, looking much more like the woman he was used to seeing—before he began building the addition, Gertie's visits, and the annulment mess.

"What?" Rose put her hands on her hips, answering Levi.

Levi ran to her. "I skated backward, *and* I made a complete circle while skating. Like this—" He backed up, sliding his feet as if he were on skates. Then he spun around. "I didn't even fall . . . not that time."

Rose smiled at him with pride. Joel removed his coat, scarf, gloves, and boots.

Levi wrapped his arms around her waist. "You said I'd get it if I kept trying." He looked up. "And I did."

"I can't wait to see it with my own eyes." Rose pinched his chin. "Hungry?" She glanced to Mose and Grace.

The answer was a resounding and loud *ya* from each one.

"Good." Rose helped Grace out of her coat. "You boys peel out of those wet clothes. Food is waiting on the table."

"It's waiting?" Mose's eyes grew wide. "How'd you do that?"

She laughed. "It's magic, or I planned ahead and then spotted you coming across the yard."

"I say it's magic." Grace sat in a chair and held out her feet for someone to pull off her boots. She had on long johns under her dress, both of which were wet from the snow.

"What are we having?"

"As many of everyone's favorite Christmas Eve dishes as I could bake since arriving home this morning."

"Ham, yams, and my favorite mac-and-cheese casserole?" Mose asked.

"Absolutely."

"Yes!" Mose danced about as he changed clothes.

Joel and Rose helped all three peel out of their wet clothing and put on dry garments. Each child, including Grace, was pretty independent when not bundled up, hungry, and tired. Soon all three were running toward the table in house shoes and dry clothes.

Rose lingered, and Joel remained in the mud room with her. What had changed?

She stepped closer, wrapped her arms around his waist, and rested her head against his chest. "I'm sorry."

"Nee. None of that." Joel embraced her, holding tight. *"Ich denk du bischt die bescht, mei sweet Rose."*

She snuggled closer. "I think you're the best too."

Joel's heart skipped a beat, and he leaned back, trying to see her.

She looked up. "Well, I do."

"Okay." That wasn't what caught him off guard. She hadn't brushed off his feelings toward her. Was she trying to stay in the moment, or did she believe him?

She grinned, looking completely at peace. "It's been a miraculous Christmas Eve."

"How miraculous?"

"Well, I have some questions for you, but whatever the answer, you won't return to the doghouse after Christmas."

"I should take the children out for the afternoon more often."

"That's not what did it. Erma came by."

Joel stared at her, stumbling back a bit. "The miracle isn't that she's buried under the fresh snow, is it?"

Rose laughed. "Nee." She took him by the hand, pulling him toward the kitchen. "We'll talk about it after the children are down for the night."

Joel tugged on her hand, stopping her. "What questions?"

"Now? Aren't you hungry?"

"I was, very much so. But curiosity chased it away. What questions?"

"You want to continue toward us having a real marriage, but you also mentioned that I had the right to choose about our marriage if the church leaders said it could be annulled. If I decided to leave, then what?"

His heart jolted, unsure whether to be pleased with the conversation or terrified. "The worst thing that could happen is that you'd leave me, but I thought you'd stay in Forest Hill because the children are here. And then I hoped you'd let me court you and win you over the old-fashioned way with more romance and less housework."

"Ya." She chuckled. "I can see you coming up with that plan. It's not happening, but I get it."

His chest pulsated with the crazy rate of his heartbeat. "What is happening then?"

"I understand now why you did what you did, why you wanted to wait to tell me about the annulment. But the conversation between the church leaders is irrelevant. Your Daed's intentions were good but unnecessary. I choose you, this marriage, and—"

Joel wrapped her in his arms and kissed her the way he'd been wanting to for way too long. He took a few steps forward while holding her, and soon her back was against a wall. His breathing was labored as he kissed her neck. "Tell me I'm awake this time."

"I can't. I'm too busy hoping for the same thing."

"Mama!" Grace called. "Levi spilled milk all over the table and floor."

"The good news is"—Joel put his forehead on Rose's, inhaling the scent of her—"their mess means we're awake."

Rose put her lips on his again, lingering. "When I wake on Christmas morn, you better be holding me."

"Guaranteed, Rose," he mumbled while kissing her. "Guaranteed."

She pulled away. "Kumm."

"We're fine right here." He put his hands on the wall on either side of her, blocking her. "That spilled milk isn't going anywhere."

"I bet it's spreading like melting snow." She ducked under his arm and scooted away. "Kumm. We have much parenting to do before we can be lovers." She held out her hand to him. "I did some work on the bedroom while you were out, and we'll spend our first night together there. I made a nice pallet using sleeping bags, blankets, and comforters."

"Perfect." Joel would never stop being awed at why God had brought the uniqueness of Rose into his life. He couldn't wait to see how much the Christmas lights she'd insisted on glowed around his angel as they spent their first night together.

He had certainly never deserved her. But he intended to try to be worthy of her love for the rest of their lives.

Double Chocolate Cheesecake

24 Oreo cookies, crushed (makes about two cups)
1/4 cup butter, melted
4 8-ounce packages of cream cheese, softened
1 cup sugar
2 tablespoons flour
1 teaspoon vanilla
2 4-ounce bars Baker's semisweet chocolate, melted
and then cooled
4 eggs
1/2 cup blueberries

Preheat oven 325°. Mix Oreo crumbs and butter, and press into the bottom of a 9″ x 13″ cake pan lined with foil. Bake 10 minutes. Beat cream cheese, sugar, flour, and vanilla with a mixer until blended. Add chocolate and mix well. Add eggs one at a time, beating on low speed after each egg, just until blended. Pour mixture over crust. Bake 45 minutes or until center is almost set. Cool to room temperature. Then refrigerate for at least four hours. Use the foil to lift the cheesecake from the pan. Top with berries.

Italian Cream Cake

$1/2$ cup butter, softened
$1/2$ cup shortening
2 cups sugar
5 large eggs, separated
1 tablespoon vanilla
2 cups all-purpose flour
1 teaspoon baking soda
1 cup buttermilk
1 cup coconut, flaked

Nutty Cream Cheese Frosting
1 cup pecans, chopped
1 8-ounce package cream cheese, softened
$1/2$ cup butter, softened
1 tablespoon vanilla
1 16-ounce package confectioner's sugar, sifted

In a large mixing bowl, beat butter and shortening at medium speed with electric mixer until creamy. Gradually add sugar, beating well. Add egg yolks, one at a time, beating until blended after each addition. Then add vanilla and blend well. Combine flour and baking soda, then add to butter mixture alternating with buttermilk, beginning and ending with the flour mixture. Beat at low speed until blended after each addition. Stir in coconut. Beat egg whites until stiff peaks form and then fold into batter. Pour into three greased and floured 9″ round cake pans. Bake at 350° for 23–25 minutes or until wooden pick inserted into the center comes out clean. Once removed from the oven, place pans on wire racks for ten minutes. Then remove the layers from pans and cool completely on wire racks.

For the frosting, place pecans in a shallow pan and bake at 350° for five to ten minutes, or until toasted. Stir every two to three minutes. Cool. Beat cream cheese, butter, and vanilla at medium speed with electric mixer until creamy. Add confectioner's sugar, beating at low speed until blended. Beat at high speed until smooth. Stir in pecans. Frost cake.

* Carol Steele James, *Feed My Sheep,* www.Facebook.com/FeedMySheepCookbook/. Used by permission.

Acknowledgments

To my publishing family—the parent company Penguin Random House and the imprint WaterBrook Press. You've supported me faithfully and thoughtfully for ten years. Thank you.

To Shannon Marchese, my editor for ten years. Equally important as the many things I mentioned in the dedication for this book, I thank you for a decade of hearing me and intervening so that I've been blessed to work with Carol Bartley.

To Carol Bartley. Thank you! From my debut novel to my nineteenth book, you've been my trusted copy and line editor, a skillful, gentle corrector, and a wonderful, thorough fact checker. I'm awed and honored that I've had the pleasure of working with you for a decade! And I'm very glad you enjoy my zany humor that strikes time and again as we hone each other's work.

To my son Tyler and my daughter-in-law Erin. Without your encouragement, help, and wonderful skills, I couldn't have completed the last two fiction books. Thank you.

And to Catherine King, a one-time reader of my books and now a wonderful brainstorming partner. Thank you!